Also by Tanita S. Davis

MARE'S WAR
Winner of the Coretta Scott King Honor Award

★**"Absolutely essential reading."**
—*Kirkus Reviews*, Starred

"*Mare's War* chronicles a part of our history
that is seldom written about
but compelling to discover."
—*The Christian Science Monitor*

A LA CARTE
"As delightful and fulfilling as the
handwritten recipes in progress included
at the end of each chapter."
—*Kirkus Reviews*

HAPPY
FAMILIES

HAPPY FAMILIES

BY
TANITA S.
DAVIS

ALFRED A. KNOPF
NEW YORK

THIS IS A BORZOI BOOK PUBLISHED BY ALFRED A. KNOPF

Visit us on the Web! randomhouse.com/teens

Educators and librarians, for a variety of teaching tools, visit us at
randomhouse.com/teachers

Library of Congress Cataloging-in-Publication Data
Davis, Tanita S.
Happy families / by Tanita S. Davis. — 1st ed.
p. cm.
Summary: In alternating chapters, sixteen-year-old twins Ysabel and Justin share their conflicted feelings as they struggle to come to terms with their father's decision to dress as a woman.
ISBN 978-0-375-86966-2 (trade) — ISBN 978-0-375-98457-0 (ebook) — ISBN 978-0-375-96966-9 (lib. bdg.)
[1. Transgender people—Fiction. 2. Fathers—Fiction. 3. Twins—Fiction. 4. Brothers and sisters—Fiction.] I. Title.
PZ7.D3174Hap 2012
[Fic]—dc23
2011026546

The text of this book is set in 11-point Goudy.

Printed in the United States of America
May 2012
10 9 8 7 6 5 4 3 2 1

First Edition

For Jacqueline, who once was Jack. And for all of us who once were blind, but now see.

BEFORE

The Phoenix Fire Festival at The Crucible, last May

Ysabel

The surge of chattering, pointing, gawking people pours into the massive auditorium, and I feel a shiver crawl up my arms. Rather than stand here, watching the watchers, I'm going to do some torchwork.

There's a table set up at the back of my booth, covered with a square of galvanized metal and lit with a desk lamp. At the edge of the table there's a small glass kiln, a miniature propane blowtorch, a handful of tweezers, metal rods, a graphite block, and a couple of terra-cotta flowerpots filled with sand and rods of glass in all shades. I sit down, my foot automatically moving to tap the switch for the small fan under the table. Checking to make sure my glasses are still on my head, I grab my box of matches and light my torch.

An older couple approaches my booth but instead of speaking I pick up the thin metal mandrel and turn it in the flames to warm it. The glass always sticks better if the mandrel is warm. My hands hover over the glass color choices, and I select a clear, bright blue. As I reach up to tug down my pink-tinted sunglasses, they catch on my hair, and the pins Grandmama put in the French roll she thought would look so elegant poke into my scalp. Muttering under my breath, I gently untangle the glasses and put them on, then start heating the glass. In no time at all, I'm putting down a small bead of molten glass, turning my mandrel until I've made a disk. I make another disk, a half inch away, and then, turning the mandrel all the time, keep laying disks of glass until the heat slumps them together to make a hollow bead. One down, a few hundred to go. I set the mandrel and the bead into the annealing kiln to slow-bake and choose another rod of color. I want something with a streak of metal in it this time.

All of us have been awaiting this last weekend in May and hoping for good weather for the thousands of people expected to attend the Phoenix Festival. It's a massive, three-day fund-raiser fair with food—spicy and cooked over an open flame, of course—face painting, flame throwing, fire juggling, fire archery, and pretty much all the firemen in three counties standing around looking worried. For me, the art show is the best part, and every one of the student artists at The Crucible has been working like crazy to get enough pieces for the exhibition. Around me are the end results—long tables covered with blue cloth displaying pottery, ceramics, jewelry, sculpture, metalwork, and of course, my glass torchwork. At the back of the hall, shelves rise to the ceiling, laden with hundreds of colorful glass vases and ornaments. Some of the largest projects (done by the blacksmiths) are on the floor at the back. Nearest my table is a sundial made out of granite with bands of brass and copper, a fused glass fountain, and something bizarre that looks like it was made out of a bicycle lit with a confused tangle of neon tubes. At the edge of each table is a binder with small pictures of each piece, listing price and artist.

I'm pretty sure no one is going to buy anything of mine today; after all, this is my first serious show. Somewhere in the crowd, though, are five judges from the Fallon School of Art & Design, and not only are the best exhibitors going to be invited to submit a few things to a juried show, but three lucky people are going to be considered for scholarships. They start the selections tonight.

At almost fifteen, I might be worrying too early about college scholarships, but this year I've decided I might as well get people used to seeing my stuff and hearing my name. The fact is, I'm not going to get into a college based on academics. I've got a B– average, but I'm not interested in setting the Ivy League world on fire, like my brother, Justin, will. This is what I do best.

My twin appears as if my thoughts have pulled him to me. "What's up, Ys?" Justin comes around the edge of the booth and steps over my tools to give me a careful fist bump. "You sold out yet?"

I grin. "Yeah, right. Four minutes after the doors open."

"You never know. Met the judges yet?"

I shudder. "I don't even want to think about judges."

Justin's phone buzzes, and he flips it open briefly. "My woman's here. Gotta go."

I smirk. "Better not let Calli hear you call her that. Thanks for showing up, Justin."

"Couldn't miss your first show," my brother says, giving me a light tap on the head. He waves and vanishes back into the crowd.

I choose a rod of clear glass and begin another bead. This time, I make a basic bead, then, after some thought, choose a rod of yellow and begin to melt little blobs of yellow against the clear. My shoulders relax, and the roar of strangers' voices turns into meaningless background music. I hum a little song to myself and rotate my blob of glass through the blue-white flame as the lumps of glass slump and the bead turns smooth again. I nod, satisfied with the effect, and then find a rod of cobalt with a spiral of silver in it.

"Ysabel!" I glance up and flinch as I see a camera. It's only Starr, the program director here at The Crucible, so I stick out my tongue and keep working. Despite the fact that I told them not to come, I *know* my parents are out there, somewhere, with Poppy and Grandmama and my best friend, Sherilyn, in the orange and red poppy sundress she told me she'd wear just to be sure I could spot her. Ms. Wendth, my old art teacher, was invited, and Justin is probably still in the building if his girlfriend, Callista, hasn't dragged him off into a dark corner somewhere.

It's a good feeling to know that all of my people are here today.

"Miss?" The older couple waves to catch my attention, and one of them says, "Did you make that pink necklace, with the big millefiori beads? How much for it?"

"Why don't you take a look at the binder there, and I'll be

right with you," I call, quickly setting the mandrel in a holder. Being taken from the heat so fast, the surface glass on my bead will probably crack. If I can't smooth the cracks with heat, I'll have to scrap it and start over again, but right now I don't care. My heart is thumping, and I wipe my sweaty hands on my jeans. It's my first sale, and I do an internal happy dance.

Thank you, thank you, thank you, God!

By the time the day is over, I've sold all but five necklaces, made thirty good beads at my station and fixed the cracked one, done a little welding at a welding exhibit, and gone outside to grab lunch and watch the fire-breathers dance. Farida, the welding instructor, came by to point out the judges from Fallon, and they've walked by slowly three or four times. I pretend not to notice.

When Starr climbs on her makeshift stage and quiets the crowd for the announcements from the Fallon judges, I cheer for the people who are being selected for the juried show. Then Starr is pointing at me, a little manic grin on her face.

"Ladies and gentlemen, tonight we'd also like to introduce our prodigy at The Crucible, Ysabel Nicholas, a freshman at Medanos Valley Christian Academy!" she shouts into the mic, and over the applause, she yells, "Stand up, Ysabel!" and I feel like I've been struck by lightning. On suddenly shaky legs, I stand, wave, and immediately hunch back onto my stool.

Starr gestures at me frantically to stand again as the group of judges comes toward my table. All of them shake my hand and say something nice. A woman with a blond-frosted afro and a massive silver and turquoise medallion hanging around her neck beams at me, and I'm almost blinded by her grin. She shakes my hand and says, "Great job, young woman!"

7

"On behalf of The Crucible," Starr says as she puts a small glass phoenix in my hands, with its wings outstretched and curlicues of glass flames beneath it. She gives me a hard hug, and I can only grin. Suddenly my family is visible at the front of the crowd, and Dad and Justin are directly in front of me. With a carefully choreographed move, the two of them lift up bouquets of roses and toss them. At my feet. In front of everyone.

I can't decide if I should laugh or run. I put my hands to my face and groan.

It's not possible to die of embarrassment. But as I hastily scoop up the bouquets and scuttle back to my seat, to the amusement of everyone around me, I'm almost positive you can at least have a coronary, or a stroke or something.

"It could have been worse," Mom says, tucking me against her side as we walk out into the parking lot. With my boots on, I'm almost as tall as she is. "Your poppy wanted us all to throw the roses one by one. I reminded him that your father and I didn't have the insurance to cover the potential breakages and eye injuries."

"Think of it this way," Sherilyn says, grinning. "The next time you get that many roses, you'll be doing a solo show. This is just practice."

"A solo show. I wish," I say, watching as Dad stands the hard-sided pink case that holds my torches and glass behind the driver's seat in Mom's van and closes the door securely. For tonight, she's removed the Wild Thyme Catering magnetic signs from the doors, and I'm glad. She gives me one last squeeze, then heads for the driver's seat. Sherilyn hops in the passenger side, and I slide in back, next to my case, and lean forward between the front seats. We've done this so many times, we all three go to our spots without any thought.

"See you at home," Dad says, and we wave as he and Poppy join Justin and Grandmama at his car.

"So, did you see the cute blacksmith instructor?" I ask Sherilyn. "Levi?"

"Ysabel, he's, like, thirty," Sherilyn complains. "What's with you and the geriatrics?"

My mother laughs, a particularly loud hoot, and shakes her head. "Geriatrics?"

"Well, just because he doesn't have fangs or skin that sparkles," I strike back, teasing Sherilyn about her latest vampire romance craze. "Levi might be thirty, but at least he's alive."

"Don't knock the vampires," Sherilyn says defensively. "You know they'd be way more mature than any guys *we* know."

"Mature, Sherilyn? Really? Let's just say *ancient*."

Sherilyn and I keep laughing about nothing in particular as my jitters dissolve. By the time we get home, I'm starving and just about on the verge of collapse. We could have stayed at the Phoenix Festival and eaten there, but I know my parents have something better planned. Sure enough, as soon as I come into the house, I can smell it. In the dining room, a pan of stuffed mushrooms sits over a chafing dish, and I head straight for the table and pop one into my mouth, savoring the garlic-and-cheese stuffing.

Sometimes it's really great to have a caterer for a mother.

"Madam?" Poppy, Mom's dad, motions me back to the door. Now swathed in a long apron over his black suit pants and white shirt, he holds out his arm to Sherilyn like a waiter, his silver-lined hair giving him an elegant appearance. "Your wrap?"

I kick off my boots and scrunch my toes in the wool rug in the entryway as Mom hurries into the kitchen, checking on all of the things she has prepped. "It's just a little bit of this and that," she explains apologetically to Sherilyn as she reappears carrying a platter of fresh veggies and dip, "but these are Ysabel's favorites."

"It looks great," Sherilyn says, examining the spread on the candlelit table.

"Mom, yum! You made a torta!" I cry, mouth watering as I see the thin layers of pesto, potato, goat cheese, and bell pepper. "Yes!"

"And deviled eggs, and corn cakes," Grandmama adds, bringing out a pitcher of iced tea, "just so we could be sure to have no theme to this meal whatsoever."

"But it's what I wanted," I sigh, reaching for another mushroom. "It's exactly what I wanted."

"Belly-Bel, can't you wait for the blessing?" Dad asks, swatting at my hand.

"Well, let's pray already!" I exclaim, dodging him and snagging another bite.

When Dad calls me Belly, I don't say, "Don't call me that," as I usually do. Tonight, I don't care if Dad drags up all of my baby nicknames. I have everything I want right now, everything I need.

"People, I have things to do," my brother announces, coming down the stairs. He's changed into his blue *Humpty Dumpty Was Pushed* T-shirt and jeans. "Let's eat."

"Justinian," my mother sighs, and Justin rolls his eyes. Though he's only six minutes younger than I am, sometimes my brother just seems like he's six. He's this huge brain and all, but occasionally he has zero social skills.

"What? I'm hungry!"

"Can't you at least greet our guest of honor?" Poppy asks reprovingly.

Justin snorts. "Sherilyn doesn't count as a guest."

"You know that's not what he meant," my mother murmurs, swatting my brother with the flat of her hand. He glares at her, then turns to me with exaggerated attention.

"Greetings, Ysabel, beloved Twin of Awesome Artistic Ability. Hey, Sherilyn, Mom; hi, Grandmama, Poppy, and Dad. Can we eat now? Finals are in three weeks and I've got papers out the wazoo."

Dad snorts, cupping his hands to disguise it. He coughs. "Justin . . ."

"What? I could have said something worse."

"Oh, spare me that," Grandmama mutters, rubbing her forehead. She eyes Justin's smirk and raises the back of her hand to him mock threateningly.

"I'm ready," Mom says, sliding a covered dish onto the table and wiping her hands.

Dad puts his long-fingered hands on my shoulders and looks down at me, his brown eyes crinkling on the edges as he smiles. "I'm proud of you, Belly," he says softly. He raises his head and smiles around the table as we all join hands. "Everybody ready? Then let's pray."

As my father's voice rumbles out behind me, I open my eyes a crack and look around the table at my mom, who is still wiping her already-clean hands on the dish towel she was carrying; at my brother, who actually looks peaceful, standing between our grandparents, holding Grandmama's hand; and at Sherilyn, whose hair is hanging forward, shielding her face while she chews

11

the mushroom she snitched. Even without a whole bunch of aunts and uncles or a second set of grandparents like most people have, my family, including Sherilyn, is complete. I close my eyes again and exhale, feeling my shoulders droop as my muscles relax.

I love this feeling, of having done a good job, of being nice and tired and faced with amazing food and all the people that I love. If I could, I'd put us all in a snow globe and keep everything as good as it is, right now, to hold on to when I need it.

"Amen," says Dad, and around the table we echo the word.

I whisper it again. *Amen. So let it be.*

Medanos Valley Senate Debate Finals last May, 2:14 p.m.

Justin

"Alacrity. Conciliatory. Ineffable."

"So, you ready for this, Justin?" Andre Wang's white shirt and suspenders suddenly loom in front of my face, blocking my view.

"Move." A halfhearted shove gets him out of my way so I can continue to study my reflection in the mirror in the green room backstage of our school auditorium. I look myself in the eyes and drop my chin, trying to appear like a confident news commentator. I deepen my voice and continue to enunciate from the list of SAT vocabulary words taped to the mirror.

"Mitigator. Penurious. Recrimination. Salvageable."

"I don't know how that's supposed to help," Andre comments, slouching against the wall and crossing his arms. With the navy and yellow bow tie he's wearing and his black hair all gelled into place, he looks like some weird old-school politician. "Reciting SAT vocab won't do crap for your interpretive event. You've got forty minutes before you even get your topic."

I roll my eyes at the short junior. "Wearing that Kentucky Fried bow tie and those suspenders won't do crap for your interpretive event, and yet, every single tournament, you show up in them."

"And I win," Andre reminds me smugly, his dark eyes narrowed. "You know I do."

"And so do I." I shrug. "So, don't mess with what works, right? Lester says I should read this stuff to keep my brain focused, so I'm reading. There are six thousand two hundred and twenty-eight SAT vocabulary words, and I'm going to blow through all of them before the year is out. I'm going to ace my SAT *and* blow your skinny butt out of the water on the interpretive event today."

"Dream on," Andre snorts. "You seen Raymond?"

"Lee's around," I mutter. *Unfortunately.* If possible, Leland Raymond is a bigger pain in the butt than Andre. As senior class pastor and chair of the student senate, he's kind of a big deal at Medanos. He's nice enough on the surface, always slapping me on the back and saying he's glad I'm on the team, but he's basically just a big act. I'm only a freshman, and I can tell he couldn't care less about me, but when Mr. Lester's around, he's my very best friend.

He wouldn't be so bad if he wasn't so . . . serious. He makes a big deal out of praying before every single event, as if God could possibly care whether Medanos Valley Christian beats out Walnut Academy in a Lincoln-Douglas debate. He takes all of his stats, all of our points and stuff, way too personally. He's not even satisfied if we win, and he's also really quick to point out any mistakes he thinks any of us have made. Last week, he even said, "There is no *I* in *team*," and he was *wasn't joking*. Mr. Lester is always telling him to ease up, but Lee's just not an "ease-up" kind of guy. Fortunately, neither am I. I've been able to keep out of his way so far.

A moment later, Lee, along with fellow senators Missy Girma, Diane Edwards, and Elena Melgar, wander in. Diane, fluffing up her curly blond hair, has her usual can of energy drink, its caffeine-and-sugar-rich formula she claims to be the secret to her speed-talking abilities.

"Where's Mr. Lester?" Missy asks, straightening the scarf around her long braids.

"Not here yet," I say, pulling my list of words from the mirror before anyone else can comment on it. "He had to pick up his kid from day care or something."

"Seriously?" Diane looks tense. "Medanos is hosting; how can he not be here? We've got fifteen minutes before we're on."

"He'll get here." Elena shrugs, adjusting her ponytail and looking unconcerned. "He always does."

"Picking up his kid." Lee rolls his eyes. "And his wife couldn't do that? You can see who wears the pants in *that* family."

I wince, thinking what Mom would say to that. All the girls take a breath, but Missy speaks first, her mouth twisted in scorn. "You are such a pig, Lee," she says, her eyes narrow. "Only you could be so full of yourself."

"What, it's not *macho* to pick up your own kid?" Elena adds, hands on her hips.

I'm not surprised to see how fast Lee backs down. "I was just joking," he complains. "Don't get so uptight, people."

"Uptight? You're the one complaining Lester's not here yet," Andre points out.

Missy just freezes Lee out again with one of her ice-eyed glares.

Mr. Lester arrives just about the time Lee's got us all gathered for a team huddle and prayer. He throws down his briefcase and jacket and rushes over to us. I'm relieved, but I try not to show it, as I feel his hand on my back. I give him a nod. I'm ready for this.

There's only time for a few quick instructions and then it's showtime. We troop into the auditorium for the first event, the team debates, for which we'll get forty-five minutes each. Leland, Elena, and Diane are up first, and I'm half disappointed, half relieved that it isn't Andre, Missy, and me. Sitting in the front row, my back to the packed auditorium, I can feel sweat prickling faintly in my armpits, and it's hard to know if it's nerves or eagerness.

The judge, an anonymous-looking blond woman in a dark suit, introduces herself, states the topic, and sits down. Relief floods through me as I hear that the opposite team has to debate against the resolution that the federal government should change its policies toward India. Obviously, we got the easy side of this question. I study the competition for this round, two boys and a girl from Calvary Chapel High School. In their uniform of navy blazers and white tops, they look take-no-prisoners professional. Lee's white shirt and dark tie, Elena's red sweater and white blouse, and Diane's black turtleneck look less put together somehow, and I have my first moments of worry. Calvary's first speaker is actually really good, and her opening arguments are sound. I find myself taking notes along with Lee and Diane, even though I won't be able to pass them to Elena for the rebuttal.

Despite some of the best persuasive speaking I've heard, and what I thought would be an easy topic, our team loses by a single point. The girl from Calvary Chapel turns out to be not just good, but brilliant. Diane is sucking down another drink, and Lee is pale and tense, but it's only the first event, Mr. Lester reminds us, and everyone has done well.

"It's up to you, Nicholas," Lee says, cornering me during the ten-minute intermission. "Wang's going to blow away the team event, but we need you in the individual."

"The individual doesn't go for team points," I remind him, keeping loose in spite of wishing I could clock him one. Why is he piling on the pressure?

"You're right, it's not team points, but good individual stats makes Medanos look good overall. Pointwise, we can blow away Valley Jewish Day School and Calvary. Now, Diane's got some good chops, but you're the freshman everybody watches. We're counting on you."

I just grunt, tuning out Lee's lame attempt at a pep talk. I watch a group of event adjudicators standing together, discussing the last event and setting up for the next one. I see my sister right in the second row, scoping out the competition, her black boots propped up on the seat in front of her. She catches me watching and gives me a thumbs-up.

Dad's out there in the crowd somewhere. He was on a business trip, but he said he'd come straight over from the airport. Mom would have been here, but her driver called in sick this morning, so she's one short at her catering company. The family always shows up at my events, which is more than a lot of guys can say. I know I'm lucky.

"So, you're ready, yeah?"

I pull my wandering attention back. "Yeah, yeah, Lee. I'm ready."

"Good man." He slaps my back and I roll my eyes.

Lee talks up this big "go, team" thing, but it's not about the team at all. It's about Lee Raymond. He really wants to walk away from Medanos and be able to say he was a *somebody* here, a big man who got things done. Whatever. It's his ego-happy moment, and it doesn't have anything to do with me.

My eyes skate back over my SAT words and I ignore them, opting to close my eyes and focus on relaxing instead.

I like forensics. I love the watertight logic of a good argument, the clarity of a strong rebuttal. I like to think fast and talk faster, and I can see going into law like Poppy, but I won't be some kind of single-minded jerk about it. There's got to be a way to be a winner and still be a decent human being. Like Dad, for instance—his new job is intense. He's in charge of building million-dollar labs for scientists and bioengineers, and he's on the road at least two weeks out of the month. Even though he has hundreds of people who answer to him, Dad's not on some ego trip. I respect him for that, for making time to go running or hang with us when he can. I want to be just mellow like that.

A flash of red catches my attention, and I see my girlfriend, Callista Douglas, sitting with her people. They've been waiting for me to look, and now each of them holds up a piece of red construction paper and flips it over. JUSTIN NICHOLAS ROCKS!! The words are in silver ink and glitter glue. My face goes into a big, stupid grin without my permission, but I duck my head, my face burning, when I hear Andre snort. I know I'm going to be hearing about my "fan club" for the rest of the year. When I look again, Callista is laughing, and my stupid smile comes back. We've only been dating for a month, but so far, it's amazing.

"Your family's here, right, Justin?" Missy looks over at me. "That lady in the white suit looks enough like your dad to be your aunt. She's got the Nicholas nose and everything."

"She's not a Nicholas, unless Dad has secret relatives he never told us about." I laugh, but the lady in the back row does look familiar. I scan the crowd, frowning. "My dad's coming. He always wants to check out my future lawyer skills."

Missy grins. "Better be impressive," she warns me.

"Always." I raise my eyebrows and try to look confident. Missy laughs and goes back to her notes. Andre looks calm and poised, in spite of his whack tie, and though I'm the only freshman, the weakest link on the team, I know I'm more than able to do my part. I get on my game face and nod. We've got this.

AFTER

Saturday, 5:28 p.m., a year later

Ysabel

It's not like Mom to want to go to the five-thirty service with us, but instead of pulling up to the yellow line on the curb, she drives the van around the oval and parks.

As she takes the keys from the ignition, I give her a look. "Um, Mom. You know Cory Vick's band is doing music tonight, right?"

A ghost of her old smile appears as she straightens the collar on her sleeveless white blouse. Tugging to adjust the drape of her pale blue slacks, she says, "That boy's drums don't scare me, Ysabel."

"O-kay." I smirk, opening my door. "But don't say I didn't try to warn you. Poppy said last time he was deaf for a couple of hours after."

"Your poppy is old," my mother says loftily, and I have to laugh.

"I dare you to say that to his face."

"No, thanks." Mom's expression is wry. She turns back to the car. "Come on, Justin."

Justin sighs heavily and doesn't move. He and my mother exchange a long, silent look, communicating any number of things, and then she slams the driver's side door, walks to the front of the van, and waits.

There's a click, then the passenger door on the far side rolls open. Long-armed, tall, and wiry, my brother, Justin, nonetheless gets out like he's a hundred and thirty, then slams the sliding door hard enough to rock the whole van. I flinch, the sound startling new pain from the headache I already had, but Mom doesn't move.

How long does it take someone to walk around a car? Impatiently, I shift forward, ready to walk into the church alone, but my mother reaches for my hand, and I wait, letting her hold me in place.

Finally Justin slouches toward us, his hands shoved in the pockets of his jeans, his shoulders hunched and his face turned toward his battered deck shoes. Mom loops her arm in his, as if his sullen silence is an invitation, and together the three of us walk into the foyer.

It's weird to be here. Lately if I show up to evening service at all, it's by myself, since this isn't Grandmama's, Poppy's, or Mom's thing, and Justin hasn't been to church now for . . . weeks. Since

Dad's been gone, Mom hasn't made a big deal out of us going, but for whatever reason, today she just put her foot down. "It's a *family* service," she'd said, and dragged us all with her.

We know why, of course. It's because we're going to Dad's house in Buchannan, and Mom's wrapping us both in an extra layer of God.

Which we might not need—no offense to God—if she'd *just let us stay home*.

My mother is the one making us spend our spring break on the other end of the state, out of touch with our friends and out of reach of anything real. I could put in so many hours at The Crucible with a week free of school, but no, she's on this thing where she keeps saying, "A daughter needs her father." Um, *hardly*. What this daughter needs is her blowtorch, thank you. Disconnected from my routine, from the steadying chaos of The Crucible, I'll be completely out of sync with myself. In the six months since Dad's been gone and everything's been so weird, routine is what I need. Without it, the world is too sharp-edged, and too right up in my face, and things comes rushing toward me.

It *is* all rushing toward me. We're flying down to Dad's tomorrow.

Mom tugs on my hand questioningly, and I realize I've almost stopped walking. I pull away and cross my arms, suddenly angry with her all over again.

I hate this. I want to put this off, put Dad off, and shove spring break onto a back burner. Instead, I'm hurtling a hundred miles an hour toward this blank space in my head, a place I've dreaded so much I can't even imagine it. Dad's house. Where he now lives a life I can't even imagine.

"Well, hey, Nicholas family! Good to see you, Justin!" Maisie

Tan, our youth pastor's wife, beams at us at the door, where she's standing and bouncing her baby. Justin just grunts and barely acknowledges her, which doesn't dim her sunny smile. A moment later, he jumps and twists away from my mother, looking irritated. She must have poked him in the ribs. She has this *thing* about greeting people at church and is not above giving us little "reminders" when we forget.

To prevent a "reminder" of my own, I quickly wave at Maisie and enter the sanctuary while Mom slows to chat. I glance back and flinch from the compassion in Maisie's face as she squeezes Mom's hand and says something I don't quite hear.

Ugh. I turn away, rubbing my arms to erase the goose bumps. "Maisie knows," I mutter to Justin, feeling exposed and betrayed. "I guess Pastor Max told her. So much for confidentiality."

My brother doesn't look at me. "Mom told her."

I look back and shoot my mother an angry look. "*What?! Why?*"

Justin, having used up his fund of words for the hour, ignores me. He moves into the back row and drops to the pew like his strings have been cut. I know Mom won't let us sit back there, so I keep going, all the way up to the third row on the left, which is where we always sit.

We've attended Church of the Redeemer my whole life, so I know just about everyone, not that I feel like talking to anyone today. People wave and chatter around me, and I sit and hope for invisibility.

"Ysabel." Sherilyn appears at the end of the pew. "I didn't know you were coming."

Crap. I look up and smile vaguely, hoping she doesn't sit down. "Hey, Sherilyn."

"So, how's life?" She leans forward a bit, her expression friendly and concerned.

"Good, good. Everything's great." The lie spills from my mouth and falls flat.

For a moment, Sherilyn stands with her hands in her pockets, staring at me. My face burns, first with shame, then anger. Why can't she just leave it alone? The awkward pause lengthens, then Sherilyn clears her throat. "Great. Glad everything's okay. Guess I'd better find a seat. Good seeing you."

"Yeah. See you." I wrap my arms around my middle, hoping to squeeze away the sick emptiness that threatens to overwhelm me. *At least Sherilyn doesn't know*, I comfort myself.

It's bad enough having Pastor Max know about Dad, but I can't believe Mom talked to Maisie, too. I thought I could be normal at church at least, and pretend like nothing had changed—everybody knows Dad travels a lot for his job, so people have gotten used to not seeing him much. Now I find myself wondering if I've been fooling myself. How long has Maisie known? Do both the pastors know? Do the elders? Does everyone?

Fortunately, the panicked circling of my thoughts is disrupted by Justin and Mom arriving to shove me further along the bench. As I scoot over, Cory's sticks tap together, Karissa, Paul, and Brianna start playing their guitars, and the music kicks off.

The band is loud and fast and energetic, and I'm grateful for the distraction. It's easier to be part of a force of voices, a wall of sound singing out with everyone else, than to deal with the spew in my brain. I do my best to just focus on the words of each song and sing. And when Cory starts off a pretty decent cover of Third Day's "Sing a Song" and urges us to our feet, I've actually, for the moment, managed to set everything else aside. Even Justin's tapping his fingers on the back of the pew in front of us.

Karissa and Brianna lean in and sing harmony, totally into the music and happy, and I'm glad for them. A lot of the older members of our congregation couldn't deal with Cory wanting his band to play for regular services. For a while, there were a lot of church board meetings and drama, and people took sides. Dad was one of the people who really pushed for the five-thirty service to be less formal and basically *younger*. When the band plays, I always realize how much I miss him.

When Mom's shoulder gently bumps mine as she turns to greet the people behind us, I don't think anything of it, except to glance to my left to see if it's anybody interesting.

When I see the familiar long-fingered hands on my mother's shoulder, shock seems to suck all the air from the room, and a soundless explosion goes off in my brain.

Dad?

Jaw slack, I stare at him—and then all the blood in my body seems to drain down to my feet. Dizzy, I turn away, hot and cold and shaky.

Dad. *Here.*

I grip my brother's arm and shake it. He gives me an irritated look, then looks again, his face worried as he studies mine. "What—"

"Dad," I hiss, jerking my chin to indicate his position.

Justin's eyes widen, and he begins to turn, then stops himself. He pulls away from my arm. "I'm out," he mutters, and moves down the pew. I clutch his arm again and squeeze.

"No!" The music stops right then, so I only mouth the word

"wait." I pull my brother's arm and make him sit, whispering, "Where can you go? If you leave, he'll follow you. Or Mom will."

Justin sucks in a shaky breath, and I see him stop himself from turning around again. He scrubs his hands over his face and sits forward, his elbows on his knees. "God," he mutters, and I hope he's praying. I know I am.

They did this on purpose. We haven't seen Dad in three months and were expecting him to meet us *tomorrow*, at the airport, in a town where we don't know anyone. *Why is he here?*

On the platform, the band is really getting into it, but all I can do is sit and wonder if people will look at my father and be able to tell. Is it obvious? If I look at him again, will I see that he's . . . changed?

Suddenly the denim skirt and T-shirt I'm wearing seem too thin as shivers crawl over my skin. Has everything changed? Is he going to spend the week with *us*?

Where's he going to sleep?

The music is quieting down to the hushed, reflective tones that mean it's almost time for prayer, and for Pastor Max to give us one of his famous ten-minute sermons—which is another reason I normally like the five-thirty service. As Pastor Max heads for the pulpit, Maisie wheels the stroller filled with their sleeping son up the middle aisle and slides in at the end of our row. She smiles over at us, but I can only manage a grimace as my heart clutches in dread. Probably she sees herself as sitting with us for moral support. What *I* see is that our way out of here is now completely blocked. Mom on one side, stroller on the other, and Pastor Max just starting the last ten minutes of the service.

We're *stuck*.

I have no idea what the sermon is about. All I know is when Cory taps his drumsticks together to count time for one last song, Justin abruptly lurches to his feet and heads for Maisie's end of the pew. Maisie moves the stroller, and I make an abortive motion to rise, but feel my mother's fingers clamp down on my wrist.

"Five more minutes," she says in my ear. "You can wait that long."

I slump back and sigh, wondering if I should just go, wondering if people are watching.

The last song. The benediction. As soon as the service is over, I'm up and moving toward the front of the church. I'm not normally a band groupie, but I'm going to be one tonight. I make small talk and stand in the loose crowd around Karissa, Cory, Paul, and Brianna, watching them pack up their gear. Cory's girlfriend, Rachel, smiles over at me.

"Where's Justin these days? Haven't seen him in forever."

"Um, he's around," I say, waving vaguely toward the back of the church.

"Ysabel. We're going." My father's voice is right behind me, and I jerk at the sound. I'm not ready, but there's no more time.

"Uh, bye." I step back as Rachel waves.

My hands are shaking, and I hide them, crossing my arms. My father is standing a few feet from me, smiling slightly. I take in his appearance with a quick glance. He looks exactly the same as always, his height and build a bulked-up version of Justin's gawky long arms and legs. His bronze-dark skin contrasts with the charcoal gray of his good suit, and his dark eyes are watching me steadily.

"I like your boots," he says.

I glance down, a little smile coming before I can stop it. "Thanks." It's really too warm for calf-high combat boots, but I love them, especially the roses embroidered up the sides. I wear them every chance I get.

My father clears his throat. "It's good to see you, Bel. I missed you."

My eyes are suddenly burning. I want to throw myself in his arms and forget all this awkwardness. "Thanks," I mumble again.

My father half turns to leave, then turns back toward me. "That a new necklace?"

I run my finger along the beads on my throat. "Yeah. It's just clay."

"It's pretty, babe. You do good work."

I fiddle with the small clay rounds and shrug. Dad's always thought it's great that I'm artistic, but he doesn't normally stand around complimenting me. This is weird. I do good work? What does he want me to say?

"I know."

My father's laugh is loud, and draws the smiling attention of the people around us. "Well, all right, then. It's good you know that. Let's go."

I follow him out of the church, catching up to him as we dodge through the crowd at the door. As we step outside, his hand brushes my shoulder, and he briefly squeezes before letting me go.

My throat aches, and I open my mouth to take in little sips of air as my nose clogs with tears. I don't know what to do with these feelings. I have missed my dad *so much*. Every time he's called, I haven't been able to talk to him, and yet, I haven't been able to leave the room. Mom puts him on speakerphone, and I stay, just to hear his voice. And now, he's here. But, even though he's here, he's not . . . back, is he?

I can't stand hoping.

Mom's ahead of us, opening the door to the van. Breaking into a run, I cross the parking lot, needing a little distance. I hope Dad understands.

God, how do I do this? How do I love someone who isn't who I thought he was?

Happy Trails

Justin

It was just before our family portrait for the church directory. I was eight.

This same parking lot where I'm standing was full of cars coming and going, just like now. The church secretary had set up a little station with hand mirrors and disposable combs for those last-minute fixes before families were seated in front of the camera in the courtyard. Dad was in the tiny bathroom between the secretary's office and the senior pastor's study, leaning into the small mirror, peering at his eyes and rubbing at his lashes. I came up behind him, walking heel-toe-heel-toe in my new black shoes, and he didn't seem to notice me.

"Daddy?"

My father jerked, his hand flailing away from his eyes. A smear of black landed on his cheek. His fingers were black, I noticed, and he was clutching a thin black pencil in his hand. It was something I'd seen Mom use before.

"Justin. Buddy." My father seemed out of breath. "How ya doing?"

"Do you have an eyelash?"

"Eyelash?" he repeated stupidly, then recovered. "Oh. No, Bud, I'm fine. You ready?"

"Yeah." I grinned up at him. "Ms. Cochrane says she likes my jacket."

"It's a great jacket." My father smiled down on me. "You look like a champ."

I remember chewing on my bottom lip, watching. Daddy seemed so different that day. Nervous. I thought he was scared about having his picture taken.

"You've got something black on your cheek," I informed him, and stared as he frantically scrubbed at his face in the mirror. For the rest of the night, I watched him, worrying. Why'd he get so jumpy? Was there something wrong with taking pictures?

That family portrait is in the stairwell at Grandmama and Poppy's place, with all the others marching through the years. Every time I walk up the stairs at that house, I see my snaggle-toothed grin, Ysabel's soft, dreamy expression, Mom's professional catering smile, and Dad's startled, black-rimmed eyes, anxiety leaking from behind a shining wall of teeth.

Fear. Like a deer caught in headlights, just before the crash.

Before we realized Dad was gone, we had no time to miss him. He called us every night on his laptop, video conferencing to walk me through my algebra and discuss world history chapters with Ys and me. He actually sent us postcards—weird ones—from all the cities where he stayed. Mom was the one who missed him, who got quieter and quieter, who took more and more weekend catering gigs to fill the time he was gone. Worried about his daughter, Poppy took off one day last January and caught up with Dad on the way back from a cross-country business trip, hoping to talk him into coming home and letting one of his foremen do the traveling for a while. Then Poppy found out the secret that changed everything.

Dad wasn't . . . isn't . . . the same man. He doesn't even want to *be* a man.

Voices rise, and a steady stream of worshippers exits the church building. Leaning against the door of the van, I watch people wave, chatter, and make plans to get together later in the week. I hear my name and see my former girlfriend, Callista, smile tentatively and wave before getting into her mother's car. I give a lame wave, both glad and miserable to see her.

Man, I miss her.

The click of the van door unlocking distracts me. Mom's on her way, striding down the walkway. I slide into the backseat and slouch. So Ysabel got stuck with Dad. I feel guilty for ducking out before he could talk to me.

Better Ys than me, though.

Poppy told Mom that if he hadn't been watching Dad's hotel room, he wouldn't have even realized it was him, with the wig and all. He stood at Dad's table in the hotel restaurant and just stared at him, trying to understand. "Christopher?" he'd said, not sure he was seeing right.

"It's Christine," Dad said.

Poppy told Mom that Dad set down his butter knife and said hello to him, like it was a perfectly normal day. And Mom found out that the linen suit she'd donated to the Community Service Center wasn't as far away as she thought it was.

It's not like I've never heard of guys wearing women's clothes. I mean, every year at Halloween somebody does it, and I know there are female impersonators and stuff. But those things are just jokes. Dad's . . . serious. I looked it up online and found a huge amount of people who are seriously into the whole thing—dresses, wigs, and women's shoes. They don't just want to put on a wig for a party or something. They want to live like this, full-time.

Full-time. Like the other person they were never even existed.

I've done the research. I know some people feel like they were born with the wrong gender, in the wrong body. The GLAAD Web site says not to say Dad's a "transvestite" or a "she-male" because those words are prejudiced and derogatory and not accurate—*duh.* When he's in drag, people aren't supposed to keep calling him Christopher, but Christine, like he prefers. If he decides he wants to get surgery to change into a girl, then we say he's a transgender person, not a cross-dresser. Blah, blah, blah, thank you, Internets.

I know all the vocabulary and all the rules about what we're supposed to do to make my dad comfortable, but has anyone asked what would make Ysabel and me comfortable? No. Did anyone ask us if we even wanted this? No.

Dad told Poppy that he knew Poppy would have to tell Mom, and he thought it would be best if he didn't come back home. After Poppy came home and told us everything, I spent hours—days—praying that please, God, this wasn't happening. I read on a Web site that Ys and I are just two of thousands of kids around the world dealing with this right now, but funny thing—that just doesn't make me feel any better. No matter how many people's stories I read online, it isn't the same. It's *my* family crashing; it's *my* dad. It's *me*.

I look at the church people in the parking lot, smiling and talking to each other, and I almost want to yell out the window, "How well do you really know your friends? Nobody is who you think they are. Christopher Nicholas wants to be a woman."

My father is cross-dressing, and my sister and I are spending spring break with him.

Mom thinks we should. I just can't get my mind around why.

"Grandmama and Poppy got him from the airport. That's where he's staying." Ysabel has closed the door to my room behind her and is filling me in, almost whispering.

"Wait, they picked him up?" I spin around on my desk chair. "I thought—" *I thought Poppy and Grandmama were on our side.* I don't finish the sentence. I know my mother would say that "in a family, there are no 'sides.'"

Yeah, like *that's* even remotely true. There are always sides. Always.

"This is such bull. They planned all of this, behind our backs."

Ysabel shrugs. "Probably. But, you know how Poppy is—he always tries to be on neutral ground when there's a problem."

"Well, I wish he'd warned us."

Ysabel blows out a sigh, leaning in my doorway. "He came up for a work meeting on Friday, so he would have been here anyway. He said it was just as easy to fly back with us."

Just as easy for whom? I want to ask, but I don't bother. "So, where is he, then?"

Ysabel opens my door. "He went to get takeout from Piatti's." She makes a face. "As if anyone is even hungry." Rolling her eyes, she heads down the hall.

I turn back to my laptop, hitting the space bar to disrupt my screen saver. Since Mom caters all week long, there's leftovers galore. We rarely eat takeout from anywhere, much less somewhere fancy like Piatti's. It's a little strange that Mom's not cooking tonight—but part of me is glad she's not. Maybe Mom's not as cool with everything as she pretends.

Ysabel has left my door open a crack. I hear her boots thudding against the floor. "Mom? Are we doing anything after we eat?"

Mom's voice is closer now. "We're just having family time. Did you want to suggest an activity?"

I snort. Yeah, we have suggestions, but I'm sure Mom doesn't want to hear them.

"Do we have to have family time?"

My mother makes a little "hmph" noise, and doesn't answer. Ysabel sighs.

"I just . . . I was going to The Crucible tonight. Mom, I'm not really ready to talk about anything," she says, raising her voice slightly to be heard over the water running in the sink.

Mom turns off the tap. "That's okay. You don't have to talk," she says. "Just listen."

I kick closed my door, feeling a twist of angry joy as it slams. I might have to hear my parents' voices, but I'm done listening to anything they have to say.

The rich manicotti, stuffed mushrooms, and parmesan-topped breadsticks are cooling on the table. The huge salad with artichoke hearts and pear tomatoes barely has a dent in it. Ysabel is nibbling on a breadstick, but everyone else is about done. None of us were all that hungry to begin with. I'm still willing to eat, until I pass out or throw up. Mom said we could hold off on any discussion until our plates were clean.

Dad pushes back his plate with a sigh. "Looks like I got too much food."

Mom makes a resigned face. "You'd better take it over to Mama and Pop's when you go," she says. "I don't want that sitting in the fridge all week; I'll never eat it all."

"We could stay here and eat it," I mutter, and flinch as my father looks over at me.

"You'll have plenty of takeout leftovers to eat at my place," he says with a laugh. "I know you'll miss your mother's cooking, though."

I lean my chin on my arm, my hand blocking my father from view. "Mom?"

She gives me a weary look. "Justin, we've been over this."

Ysabel clears her throat, and I glance over at her. She's fussing with her fork, making sure it aligns with her knife just so. Without looking up at my father, she asks, "So, what are we supposed to *do* all week?"

Dad laughs shortly. "What do you do during any spring break?" he asks.

"Whatever my parents aren't doing," I mutter.

"Well, *my* plan was to be at The Crucible all week and get in some real work hours," Ysabel says stiffly. "But I guess my plan doesn't matter."

"Of course it matters. Belly, I especially went out and bought you a little propane so you can work on your small glass projects, at least," Dad says diplomatically. "As for what else we're going to do? Well, I want you to speak with some professional people I've met, and go on a couple of outings with other transgender individuals and their families—"

"Wait, what?" Ysabel looks rattled. "Dad, I don't want to hang out with . . . people."

"We read the stuff you sent us, and we looked at the Web sites," I remind both my parents while staring at Mom. "I don't think we need to *meet* anyone. That's not necessary."

My father laughs again, a humorless sound, and turns to my mother, as if expecting her to jump in. Mom quirks her eyebrows and shrugs silently. Dad rasps his hand across his stubbled chin and sighs. When he turns toward me, I look down, studying the congealing sauce on my plate.

"Not everything has to be weighed in terms of necessary and unnecessary, Justin. It's important for us to be together for a bit, to talk things through, and get comfortable with each other again. It's important for us to spend time together that isn't stressful. And I also think it's important for you to meet other transgender folks and their families." He glances at Ysabel. "Yes, they're strangers for now. But I'm hoping you can come away with a few friends."

The headache that has been hovering around the edges of my

consciousness lances me through the eye. "I still don't see why we need to meet anyone. They don't have anything to do with us."

"Justin." My mother's voice is definite. "Your father is a transgender individual, and he will always have something to do with you. We are a family, and we will stay a family."

I blow out an impatient breath. "You know what I mean, Mom."

Mom nods. "I do. But I also know that other families who have been through this type of a change might be really helpful for you to meet, to give you some insight into how things will be from now on." She pauses. "Do you understand?"

I look away. What I understand is that nothing we say is going to make a difference.

After a moment, Ysabel bursts out, "Well, I'm not looking for friends." She fiddles with her beads. "I have friends at The Crucible."

"And a week away from them won't do you any harm," Dad reminds her.

"What, now there's something wrong with The Crucible?" Ysabel exclaims. "What happened to saying I did good work?"

My father closes his eyes and pinches the bridge of his nose. "Ysabel. There is nothing wrong with The Crucible. You won't be gone for long. This is a step we need to take in putting our family back together, and you both might find that you enjoy yourself this week, if you just give yourselves half a chance."

"I get that you want us to socialize, okay," I begin, but Mom interrupts.

"We're past the point of debate, guys," she says firmly. "You're both going to go."

"Well, then, I'm so glad we had this talk," I say, pushing abruptly back from the table. "I feel much better about everything. Are we done?"

"We're leaving for the airport at seven," my father says wearily.

I grab my plate and head for the kitchen. Ysabel is only a half step behind me. I'm around the corner and halfway down the hallway before my mother speaks again.

"That went well," she says. Dad laughs, but it isn't a happy sound.

When we read *Anna Karenina* for AP English Lit this year, that thing Tolstoy says about happy families got to me. Happy families *are* all alike—all of them are safe and confident that nothing on this earth can take that away from them. Just as we were, before Dad's little secret hit us like a wrecking ball.

Now that we're one of the unhappy families, all I can do is ask the questions I should have known to ask back then. Is Dad gay? Is this something he was all along?

And if Dad wants to be a woman, do I not have a father anymore?

God hates divorce. This is what it says in the Bible. Since God hates it, my parents aren't big fans, either. From Mom and my grandparents I've heard that bit from Malachi about breaking vows and divorce so often lately I can practically recite it. "Honor thy father and thy mother" is also one of the Big Ten I learned before I was five, and I've filled up tons of notebooks and reams of paper for Bible class on what "honor" means.

Along with all the rules, I've heard enough about love to fill books. God's love is supposed to be unconditional, never changing, always there even for the worst of us, blah, blah, blah. We're supposed to love each other like that, but here's the thing: people never do.

Fact: My parents have always said that love is enough to get me through anything.

Fact: They're wrong. I love my dad, but I can't deal with him.

Fact: I'm breaking a commandment. I know my behavior isn't honoring anyone, but God really has to give me a break on this. I mean, did Dad honor us when he decided to put on high heels? Did he honor my mother when he took her clothes? Shouldn't somebody say something about fathers honoring their sons?

Paying Attention

Ysabel

Grandmama has a saying she always drags out about eavesdroppers never hearing anything good about themselves. Fact is, people who don't eavesdrop on their parents never find out anything. I *need* to eavesdrop. I have to know what Mom and Dad are thinking.

"I'll load," I hear Dad say, and Mom murmurs something in reply.

I open the door to my bedroom a little wider, straining to catch the words.

I didn't really believe it, when Mom told us about Dad. Afterward, when I thought about it, I realized what I was missing was him saying the words *It's true. I don't want to be your father anymore. I want to be a woman.* All the time Mom was talking, all I could think was, *It's a lie. All of this is a lie.*

Starr is always saying that a true artist is someone who pays attention. After Mom talked to us, I paid attention, for once, to my family. And I watched as we each tried to live with what we knew.

The blinds stayed closed, even though it was autumn and my mother's favorite time of year. She slept late, went to bed late, and walked the house at night. She wasn't that bad, though, until she had to cater an October wedding. She worked like crazy on it, spray painting pomegranates gold, gilding leaves and faux pearls for the serving tables, and making everything memorable and breathtaking and beautiful. And then, when it was over, she just . . . stopped, like somebody had pushed the Off button on the remote.

It would have been better, maybe, if she'd cried. At least she would have been *there*. Instead, for weeks, all we had was Mom's body. Her brain was someplace far, far away.

Mom's voice rises again, saying something trivial about utensils, and I move out into the hallway, just a few feet from my door. The scraping of plates reminds me of the days when Mom would dump her food in the trash and go without.

When Dad left, Mom fell out of love with food, which was, for her, like falling out of love with her life. Not even Poppy bringing her the first persimmons from his tree perked her up. After the last wedding, she couldn't even work anymore; nothing about food held her interest. And her collarbones started to stick out. By the beginning of December last year, Grandmama started showing up to fill the cupboard and cook for us.

It was hard to care about the things Grandmama fussed about, like laundry and dishes and making beds. It was impossible to sit at the table and pass the bread and talk to each other like everything was okay. I found it easier to put on my headset at The Crucible and turn off the ringer on my phone.

After Dad moved up north to some generic little town called Buchannan, it was like Justin wanted to make sure no one mistook him for the same person. He'd already dropped debate team a month earlier, but once Dad moved, he seemed to disappear. He wouldn't even answer questions like "How are you?" His friends and teachers nagged at him, and the more people tried to pull him out of himself, the quieter he got. He hardly said anything, and then what he did say was usually purposefully cruel so that people would leave him alone.

I pay attention to my brother, and I see someone who I don't know anymore.

He was always the guy who was driven and intense, who aced his PSATs and took home a trophy for the national science fair competition and won just about every spelling bee. Now he doesn't even bother to compete. He spends so much time online, Mom's not letting him bring his laptop to Dad's. He shrugged when she told him. I know he'll just use his phone.

I keep trying to tune out the chaos and focus on the future. I can't wait to get out of here. I've decided to go to college at the Penland School of Crafts in North Carolina and maybe apprentice to an artist, learn some glass technique or blacksmithing that isn't taught anymore. And then I'll make jewelry and sculpture, work on getting enough commissions to open a shop, and . . . move past this part of my life.

The clang of the trash can lid reminds me of the clash of metal on the anvil, and I think longingly of my little dedicated space at The Crucible.

Art was an interest that turned into a hobby. It is now an outlet that I *need*; it seems like the only time I feel calm and brave is when I'm playing with fire and glass and metal. My welding teacher thinks it's amazing how I've gotten so much better with accuracy and control these past few months. Levi, the blacksmithing instructor, is impressed with the challenging work I'm doing now, but Mom doesn't like how much time I'm spending with college students she doesn't know, girls with muscular biceps and tribal tattoos and sweaty, shaved-headed guys who are straight-up pyromaniacs. She always asks, "So, how's Sherilyn? How's Kate and Dannika?" It's like she can't understand that their lives are so much different than mine that what they're doing doesn't really matter anymore.

The thing is, it's easy to put people off. All you have to do is stop trying to have friends. It's easy to put the projects between myself and everyone else. *I'm helping with a bronze pour tomorrow. I have a hundred beads to make for Sherilyn's birthday present. I have a test tomorrow in trig. I'm so tired. I have a sore throat, a headache, PMS.* People know better than to ask me to do things now. I'm busy. I don't have time to talk much, not even to Sherilyn, my used-to-be best friend. But it's safer this way. It's better this way.

Footsteps make me jump back into my doorway. A door closes at the end of the hall. Bathroom. The creak of leather tells me that someone is in the living room, sitting in the rocker. Probably Dad, since that was always his favorite chair.

After a moment I hear water in the bathroom, and the door opens. The sound of cloth and the muffled ting of the couch springs lets me know it's safe to step back out into the hallway, and risk moving toward the corner. I'm still hidden but can see the edge of the fireplace and the top of the recliner.

For a while, my parents talk about general things—Grandmama's garden, Poppy's visit to some friends in Portland, whether the tires on Mom's car need to be rotated. And then Dad sighs.

"So, Stace . . . are we ready for this?"

I move closer, listening to Mom's dry laugh.

"I don't think there's any way to *be* ready for this. But we have to start somewhere."

There's a pause, and I frown, wondering what "this" could be. Dad begins again, sounding uncertain. "Look, if you want to change your mind, I'll understand. If you decide you don't want—"

"Christopher—*Chris*. You belong with us, and we belong together. We'll just take the rest a step at a time, all right?"

Silence, then Dad's voice, low and pained. "Justin can't even *look* at me."

"He loves you. You know how much he loves you. Give him time. He's just scared. It's easier for him to play his computer games than interact with the real world."

"I don't like those shooter games he plays," Dad says, his voice worried. "As angry as he's been, I don't want him to look at the whole world as a target."

"We've talked about that—he's playing something else now, a quest game, more world building and less shooting. He said he has no interest in turning out to be a statistic."

Dad gives a ragged laugh, and I imagine he is shaking his head. "At least Belly's not scared," he says, and chuckles again. "I wouldn't want to get between her and her blowtorch right now, but she seems like she's doing all right."

"Bel takes things in stride. Justin will need a little more from us, but both of them will be fine," my mother reassures him again, and I frown, feeling vaguely annoyed to be so easily dismissed.

"And what about you, Stacey?" Dad sounds sad. "You're worrying about the rest of us, but will you be fine?"

My mother hesitates. "I— That's not important now. Justin and Ysabel are my priority."

The leather creaks, and I flinch, stepping back silently.

"I understand, of course." Dad's voice is polite, free of any emotion. He clears his throat. "Well, I'd probably better get Poppy's car back—"

"No." Mom's voice is stronger. "Pop can drive Mama's car if he needs something. Stay awhile, all right? Just . . . watch TV with me or something. Read the paper. Be in the same room with me." I hear the couch springs and imagine them facing each other, imagine Mom's strained expression as she gives a painful laugh. "Every night Justin vanishes upstairs to his computer, Ysabel's over at The Crucible, and I'm rattling around in here by myself. Pick something to watch. I'll make coffee."

Is Mom that desperate? She doesn't want Dad to sleep over, does she?

"You sure?" Dad sounds tentative.

"I miss you," my mother says simply.

My breath hitches loudly in my throat, and I hurry to my room, my hand pressed over my mouth. Closing the door behind me without a telltale click of sound, I wheeze, my exhalation sobbing out of me as my heart pounds.

I miss you.

The simplicity of Mom's words is what destroys me—I miss

my dad, too. But what brings the tears is what I know now: missing him isn't enough to make him come back.

I hate weekend flights. Everyone at the airport is way too kicked back. No one is hustling off to meetings or rushing to work, and inevitably I'm stuck next to someone's crying baby on a jaunt to Grandma's house.

I also hate that we have to arrive an hour early for a flight, even though it's less than an hour by plane up the coast to where Dad is now. Finally, I hate that my mother tried to keep me from bringing my big art case with my two torches and the larger annealing kiln. It's perfectly legal to bring it, as long as it's not a carry-on, and I have the perfect place for my tools—a suitcase modified inside with a thick liner of foam, cut to the shapes of the delicate tools.

"Dad promised he'd get me propane," I argue, trying not to sound as hostile as I feel.

Mom looks at the hot-pink suitcase with the flame decals all over it and shakes her head. "I said you could do glass, but you're going to be doing a lot of other things, Ysabel. You're not going to have time to work; there's no reason for you to lug all of that with you."

"It's *my* arm."

My mother leans closer. "It's *my* concern that you're going to bring all of that stuff and just hole up in your room like you do at home."

I give her a toothy smile. "Well, if I were staying home, you could make sure . . ."

My mother rolls her eyes. "Try and have a good week, Ysabel." She kisses me and kisses Justin, and after a brief prayer for our safety, she hugs me and hugs Justin. When she puts her arms around both of us and hugs us again, Justin actually snaps out of wherever his brain has gone lately to exchange a wide-eyed look at me.

Mom's *not* the huggy one in our family. That's Dad. My mother is more likely to show her love by ranting at me when I get hurt and scare her or by shooting at me with the little purple rubber bands that come on the green onions. She's not the one who shows love by cradling my head in her hands and leaning her forehead against mine, but that's what she's doing this morning.

"Um, Mom, we're not going that far," I say finally, and her stricken expression makes me wish I had kept my mouth closed. She tries to smile, and I see the tension in her face.

"Stacey." And there's Dad, putting down his bag and wrapping her up in the kind of hug that used to make her squeak, then whack him on the shoulder and demand to be let go. But today she just stands there and buries her face in his collar.

Dad kisses her hair and whispers to her, and people look on curiously as we stand there, apprehensive and completely out of place at this tiny commuter airport with our luggage and our parents, who are obviously having a Moment. Finally Mom pulls back, smiling, as if we're supposed to be reassured by her fake happy face when her eyes are red-rimmed and glazed with tears and her nose is shiny.

"Have a good week, guys," she says thickly, and I know with utter certainty we won't.

Block Party

Justin

As soon as I hear the knock, I cut my Internet connection and shove my phone under the pillow. I turn over, my back to the door. I doubt he'll open it if I don't answer. I've been ignoring him since we got on the plane this morning. I've learned that most of the time, people leave you alone if you seriously convince them that you want to be. Like in debate, it's all in the right delivery. I've had lots of practice.

We got here about noon, and Dad showed us around his bland little town house—kitchen, dining room, living room, and master bedroom upstairs; rooms for Ysabel and me, a bathroom, and a laundry room downstairs. He pulled out bags of chips and some stuff for hoagies and told us we could settle in, then come upstairs and have some lunch and get him caught up with what we've been doing for the last few months. To which I thought, *Yeah, right*, and proceeded to throw down my bag and stretch out on the bed.

Dad knocks again, and I tune out the sound. I lie still and concentrate on a silent message: *Go away*. I lie still for so long that I actually start to doze off.

My eyes fly open and my heart slams against my ribs when something touches my shoulder. At my wild look, my sister takes a big step back, oh so casually putting herself out of arm's reach.

I wipe my mouth with the back of my hand, pretending I don't notice her reaction.

"What?" My voice is harsher than I intended.

"Dad's been asking if we want to go eat." Ysabel looks tense, waiting. Yawning, I rub my face, wondering how long I was asleep. The light coming through the window is leaving bright squares on the wall. I must have slept through lunch.

"You can get out now," I invite her, then raise my brows as Ysabel gives me a look that is equal parts hurt and irritation. It doesn't take a special twin vibe to know she's pissed.

"What?"

She shrugs stiffly. "Nothing. Just . . . you kind of stayed in here and left me with Dad."

I give her an incredulous look. "I didn't leave you with any-one. I took a nap. You could have done that, too."

Ysabel leans against the wall and shrugs. "I guess. But we were supposed to *talk* and all. Figure stuff out, like he said."

I yawn and slip my phone from under the pillow into my pocket. "Not interested. You go ahead, though."

"*Justin*." Ysabel sighs.

"Wh*at*?" I imitate her whine, shoving down the flicker of guilt I feel.

"Fine. Screw it." She flings open the door.

"Okay, okay." I put on my shoes. "Where are we supposed to have dinner?"

"How should I know? Hurry it up," Ysabel says, and slams my door.

I wince, but instead of following her, I pull out my phone and reconnect to the Internet. I squint at the Kids of Trans Web page, sign in with my username, JustC, and look at my post on the message wall. I've been lurking on the site since Dad left, reading conversations between people and finding out about their personal experiences. It always feels a little like I'm snooping, like I'm sneaking around in people's private lives, but today I realize that my private life is a lot like theirs.

Frowning down at the tiny screen, I take a breath and do something I've never done before. I post a message.

> **JustC:** Spring break, hour one: visiting the new Dad/Chris, who is now Dad/Christine.

To my surprise, I get almost instant replies.

> **Styx:** been there. done that.
> **C4Buzz:** First time. Drama!
> **Viking:** Happy first visit. Don't forget he's still the same person.

A kick at the door rattles me into snapping my phone closed before I can reply. Ysabel glares at me from the hallway, and I silently follow her upstairs, wrapped in my own thoughts.

Happy? Viking means well, but seriously—I'm not seeing cause for celebration. And is Dad really the same person? Isn't the point of this whole thing to say that he's *not?*

It's awkward in the car. Dad makes small talk while Ysabel glowers at me, still pissed at having had all of Dad's attention this afternoon. It's a relief to park the car and join the trickle of foot traffic out onto the sidewalk past the Road Closed signs to the street lined with stalls for the farmer's market.

The smell of popcorn hits me, and my stomach growls.

There are far more people than I expect: kids in face paint running around screaming, a DJ playing tunes for an impromptu dance party on the sidewalk, and booths for political candidates. The crowd noise is a dizzying assault, but I ignore my urge to run away and dive in, putting my head down and pushing, getting further from Dad and closer to the madness. Near the center of the action, I smell hot sugar, and my mouth waters. Ysabel appears beside me, and we exchange a look. Street-fair food. Funnel cake. *Dinner.* Suddenly there seems to be something worthwhile to the day. I pick up the pace and join a line a little way ahead of us. I don't care what they're selling. It smells like sugar and grease, and I know I want some.

Dad hesitates in the midst of the crowd, obviously torn between staying with me and keeping up with Ysabel, who has drifted toward a fast-moving line for some kind of pastries. In minutes, she's digging in her pocket for cash and threading her way purposefully across the road to meet me.

Impatient minutes later I meet her halfway, clutching a grease-spotted plate of crispy-hot funnel cake, covered with drifts of powdered sugar. Ys is juggling a paper container of something cinnamon-sprinkled and deep-fried. Dad, meanwhile, is approaching with a bottle of water and an expression that's half amused and half squeamish. I ignore him and take another bite of my cake.

"Whatcha got?" I mumble around a mouthful of sweetness.

Ysabel sucks in air to soothe her scalded tongue. "Gravenstein apple fritter," she says, and chews rapidly, her mouth open to sip in cooling air. "Apples, sliced, battered, and deep-fried." Ysabel dances in place and puts her hand over her mouth. "Hot!"

"Good?"

She nods emphatically, bouncing on her toes, and I roll my eyes. I envy my sister; like Mom, it seems she can section off her brain and be totally happy in a moment of food bliss, no matter what else is going on. Unfortunately, I'm too aware of my father hovering in the background to enjoy my funnel cake, which is a waste of really good fried dough.

"I don't know how you two can eat like that," Dad says, shuddering as Ysabel snitches a bite of my funnel cake, and I eat the last of her apple fritter. My father digs out his wallet and flips it open. "I'll make a contribution to the cause, but I hope you eat something that resembles real food instead of that sugar and grease."

"Don't need money." Even though I could use the twenty he's holding, I resist taking it from between his fingers, feeling my stomach clench at the idea of accepting anything of his.

"We don't need real food, either," Ysabel adds, licking her

fingers as she shrugs and Dad puts his wallet away. "We need nachos, and peach rings, and lemonade."

"I don't see nachos," I say, scanning the row of booths. "There's chili dogs, though."

"No." Ysabel frowns. "They've gotta have nachos. You can't have a street fair without orange liquid cheese squirted on tortilla chips. It's just not possible."

"You make it sound disgusting," I tell her. "And the peach rings? Are foul."

"Nobody asked you to eat them."

"Look, why don't we split up?" Dad begins, moving so he can see both of us at once. "I'll go pick up some produce, and if I see nachos, I'll text one of you. That way—" He breaks off with a grin, waving at someone. I turn to see a tall blond woman making her way through the crowd toward us. I begin to back away.

She's very tall.

"I'll find the nachos," I announce, feeling dread tighten around my throat.

She's too tall. I know women can be tall, but she's as tall as Dad. Is she a transperson? I'm not ready for this.

"Wait, Justin. Let me introduce—"

"Justin!" Ysabel hisses, her expression indignant, but panic is driving me.

"Be right back," I promise, and dive into the crowd.

Over my shoulder I see the woman shaking Ysabel's hand, probably giving her that "Your dad has told me so much about you" line. As I escape, Dad's eyes meet mine.

I know that look. It's Dad's "I'm disappointed in you" face. Yeah, well, too bad. In the last six months, there's been a lot of disappointment to go around in the Nicholas family. Unfortunately for my father, I'm immune to that face now.

Mostly.

I wander through the crowd for endless minutes, not really seeing anything. I feel like a stupid little kid, running from a strange woman. What was I so afraid of? And it wasn't cool to ditch Ysabel like that; she's already pissed at me for leaving her with Dad before.

This is Dad's fault. I already told him: I don't need to meet anyone. Why can't he just listen to me, one time?

I only stumble across the nachos by accident, and then I have to wait in a line that stretches back about fifteen people or so. Just as I take my place at the end, my phone buzzes in my pocket, and I dig it out, expecting a message from Ysabel. Instead, it's from Dad, and a moment later, my phone starts singing whatever stupid pop song Ysabel programmed in the last time she stole my phone. Nervously, I answer and blurt the first thing I can think of to defend myself.

"I found the nachos."

A pause. "All right. You in line?"

"Yeah. About ten people in front of me."

"Okay. So, head back this way as soon as you can. We'll eat near the gazebo. Think you can find it?"

"Yeah." I pause a beat, listening to the babble of voices and music on his end of the line. My fingers itch to hang up, but I know my father. He's waiting, like he always does when I owe him an apology. I try to wait him out, feeling my stomach tensing up in the silence.

"Look, about your friend, I told you I—" I begin defensively.

"Justin, do you know I love you?" he interrupts.

"What?" I look around as if others can hear our conversation. "What's that got to do with anything?"

"Do you know I love you?" my father persists. "Do you?"

"Yeah, yeah," I say hastily, not wanting him to say it again. "I know."

"Good," Dad says. "Make sure you get enough nachos for all of us."

"Yeah, I know," I say into the silence, then I frown. "Dad?"

No reply. I put the phone away with the strange feeling that I've somehow been tricked, and Dad's scored points off of me . . . but what's the game?

Sunday Night, 11:46 p.m.

Ysabel

The Myers-Briggs personality tests we took in Future and Family class say that I'm ENFJ: extroverted, intuitive, feeling, and judging. Based on that list, I'm supposed to be a leader, totally goal-oriented, decisive, and good at reading people. Justin's test was, of course, the total opposite. He's all about rules and order, figuring out what makes things tick, and making everything work.

We might have shared space before birth, but we're nothing alike.

Even the way we deal with stress is way different. It's 11:42 p.m., and Justin is sprawled bonelessly on the floor next to my bed, dead to the world. I'm sitting under the window at a table filled with a mess of glass rods, my torchwork case propped open at my feet, trying—badly—to make beads. There's no fan, but with the windows thrown open and the torch going, it's not that hot. This table is cramped, though, and the light isn't right. My mandrel was too cool, and the glass didn't stick for my first bead. The second one I took off the heat too soon. The one I'm working on now is . . . average. I was all excited about making some twisty rods for jewelry, spirals of colored glass around a core of clear. I was going to try and use them for some earrings I saw, but I can't even get started right.

I watch the glass slump into a bead shape at the end of my mandrel and carefully use the graphite paddle and my mashers to flatten it into a square. Quickly I turn a green rod in the flame, pulling a drop of what will be brass-colored glass from its molten tip and turning it onto the flat, square bead.

The colors are all wrong. The glass looks like a crooked, half-sucked lollipop. I pull it out of the fire in disgust.

Justin flops over and lets out a snore. I glance at him and sigh. As easy as it would be to push away the events of the last eight hours, sleep isn't happening for me tonight. And Justin is grinding his teeth.

After bailing on me when Dad introduced me to his friend—which I still don't get; she was just someone from work or something—Justin tried to make it up to me all evening. He brought me nachos with extra jalapeños. He tried to buy me a bracelet from a little craft stall, but it was completely overpriced and the beads were crap—there was no way I would let him pay what the guy was charging. And, just after we got home and we called Mom, he dragged his mattress into my room and brought out a deck of cards. He interrupted my plans to work, but whatever, it was nice to hang out for a change, and I beat him twice playing War.

Justin turns over again, and for a moment, there's silence.

Not that he's been doing some kind of bizarre mime thing, but tonight's been the most Justin's talked to me in weeks. We used to talk all the time. I'd be making beads at night, and Justin would come to my room with his laptop and surf weird news sites so he could read me the headlines. (*Police arrest woman buying drugs with Monopoly money!*) We'd discuss all the gossip from school, who was getting together or breaking up, and just . . . hang.

Even with all the attention he got for being the freshman anchor on the debate team, Justin still managed to be just . . . normal. Until his last debate team event.

Despite the fact that one or the other of them always shows up, somehow, neither Mom nor Dad made it to his final meet. And it was the worst timing ever. He'd had a hugely important semifinal, and he just . . . choked.

Justin's girlfriend, Callista, was sitting with a bunch of her friends for the semifinals in the row right in front of me, and she told me she thought Justin was sick. At first, he just sort of swayed, grabbed onto the podium—and then he walked off the stage. By the time I realized he wasn't just in the bathroom puking, he'd left campus, which is against school policy. Later, Mom and Dad cleared it up and told the school he was sick, but they weren't positive about that. Since I told them he threw up and he did go straight home and to bed, they bought his story.

They have no clue what happened.

I do.

I came home and found him destroying everything in my parents' bathroom, his eyes all bloodshot. He'd knocked Dad's colognes off of his vanity, broken his old-fashioned shaving mug and brush we gave him for Father's Day one year, shoved his wool suit in the toilet, and smeared Mom's makeup all over the sink. He'd written LIAR on the mirror over and over again in this really bright shade of lipstick, and when I came in, he was trying to break the mirror above the sink, just *wham! wham! wham!* Punching with his fists.

When he saw me standing in the doorway with my mouth open, he tried to say something and starting crying, making these horrible retching noises.

"What?" I'd practically screamed. "What's the matter?"

For the longest time, all Justin could say was "Dad."

By the time my parents got home, their bathroom was scrubbed, Dad's suit was folded up in a plastic bag, ready for the dry cleaner's, the mug was mended with epoxy, Justin was tucked in bed with lots of water and orange juice, and we had our stories straight. Dad might have noticed that the floor was wet and there was a big crack in his bottle of *Amour Pour Homme,* but he never said anything. He probably figured he'd bumped it too hard on the sink.

I didn't believe my brother when he told me, but this is what he said: Dad was at Justin's debate. Only, he wasn't really Dad— he was wearing a wig, and a white suit, and high-heeled shoes.

Justin met Christine before any of us.

I turn off my torch and put the still-hot glass on the graphite pads for safekeeping. As I yank off my glasses, my brother turns over and inhales. I turn off the lamp, wait a moment, then cross to his makeshift bed and look down at him. A few seconds later, Justin breathes out with a little whistling noise and starts grinding his teeth again.

I tug on his pillow.

We had a weirdly good time tonight. Even though Justin bailed on me—the punk—Dad and I met a guy who raises bees, and Dad bought some honey, then he picked out some vegetables, and we bought olive bread and some cheese to take home, and then Justin came back with three big things of nachos, lemonade, and cinnamon churros. We went to the benches at the gazebo on the corner and had a little junk food picnic.

I expected . . . something else. Some kind of confrontation. Some kind of evidence Dad was going to spring on us that let us know that everything had changed. Even Justin kept looking at Dad out of the corner of his eye, and when we got home, he was just kind of waiting, tense. And nothing happened. We called Mom and talked. Dad puttered around in the kitchen and put the food away, then he sat on the couch with the paper and the news on like he always does. At about ten, he said he'd see us tomorrow at breakfast, and then he went to bed.

And that was all.

I sigh as my brother starts grinding his teeth again. It's been a long day, my beads suck, I'm in a weird, generic town house in the middle of nowhere, and I want to try and sleep.

"Justin," I say, poking him on the shoulder.

He's awake immediately, coming up on his elbows, alert. "Ys? You okay?"

"Where's your teeth thingy?"

"What? Oh." Justin wipes the back of his hand across his mouth and sits up, grimacing. "Sorry."

"It's no big deal, but Dr. West says you're screwing up your jaw sleeping without it."

Justin sighs. "Yeah, yeah. I know." He scratches his long, skinny arms, then rolls to his feet and stumbles to the door. A few moments later, he's back, the red plastic case in his hand. He plops down on his makeshift bed and looks up at me, his eyes barely visible in the dimness.

"You okay?"

I shrug. "I guess. It's kind of quieter here than I'm used to. It didn't make sense to pack my stereo when we're only here for a few days."

"Stereo." Justin shakes his head. "Would it *kill* you to try something smaller? You're the last person in America without at least an MP3 player."

"I can't sleep with anything in my ears."

"If you're asleep, you don't feel it."

"*Whatever*, Justin."

My brother snickers. "Wow, that's a great comeback, Ysabel. 'Whatever.' You should join a debate team, you know that?"

"Shut up." I lean over the edge of the bed and whack him with my pillow, and he yanks it out of my hands. After a brief struggle, in which we basically beat each other until Justin wimps out and begs for mercy, I lie back, wheezing but victorious.

At least in my version of the fight.

When he's caught his breath, Justin breaks the silence. "Ys?"

"Yeah?"

"Seriously, though, you're okay, right?"

I nod, then realize he can't see me in the dark. "Yeah." I chew my lower lip, rolling the bedspread between my fingers. "I just . . . ?"

"Hm?"

"Just thinking about Mom at the airport."

Justin leans against the bed, his head a darker blob against the burgundy spread. "Yeah. She was . . ." Justin sighs. "This is all so messed up."

"I know. I think our being here is part of something they're doing, though. That's why she was so upset."

"What do you mean?"

I hesitate. "I don't know for sure. I mean, I just heard some things."

Justin slides his arm across the bed until he touches my leg, and then he flicks me hard with his middle finger.

"Ow! Cut it out."

"Well, stop stalling."

"Okay, fine," I blurt, rubbing the sore spot. "I think they're selling the house."

There's a tense little silence, then Justin says, "What makes you think that?"

I roll onto my stomach and lean on my elbows. "Last week, I heard Mom saying something to Grandmama about not waiting, and then, I mean, you saw how upset she was at the airport. I think Dad wants us to live here part-time with him."

"I've been erasing phone messages from Realtors." Justin's voice is dull.

"What?" I gasp, feeling chilled. "They're calling already?"

"*That's* why Mom was crying, I guess." Justin sighs. "Maybe she doesn't want to, but everybody's got to do what Dad wants now."

"Justin, that's ridiculous. Mom has a business; she's not going to pack it up just because Dad says so. And if they're selling the house, it's probably so Mom can get an apartment or something. If they're sharing custody, we'll have half our stuff here."

"I'm not staying even half-time. Mom can act like Dad's . . . clothing thing doesn't mean anything, but I'm not playing this game. We'll move in with Grandmama and Poppy. It's a long commute to Medanos Valley, but at least we wouldn't have to change schools."

"You know what Poppy said when this all started," I remind him. "He said they're going to keep out of it."

"Mom and Dad can't make us stay here," Justin insists. "It's not going to happen."

I shrug helplessly. "I just don't see that we've got any choice."

When Justin speaks, his words are garbled by his mouth gear. "Don' worry, Ys," he lisps tightly. "Just go t'sleep. Nothing's going t'happen."

Adjustments

Justin

The day Poppy came back, we all sat around the dining room table, Mom in her usual spot closest to the kitchen, Grandmama next to Poppy, their fingers knotted tightly together, and Ysabel and me across from them. I knew what this was about, and all over again I was struggling to breathe. I wanted to hear Poppy say it. At the same time, I wanted him to shove what he knew into a box, drop it to the bottom of the ocean, and never speak of it again. Just saying the words out loud would make them true. If I didn't let Poppy talk, we could pretend that none of this was happening.

It wasn't any easier for Mom. I knew Poppy had already told her and Grandmama something, but Mom was holding herself stiffly, her lips pressed together firmly and her back straight. Ysabel was sitting with her arms wrapped around herself the same way Mom was, and I realized that Mom's tension was for me and Ysabel.

For a moment, I was able to think about someone other than myself, and I felt sick. Ysabel hadn't believed me before. For her sake, I didn't want her to believe me now.

"We don't need to hear this, Poppy," I blurted, trying to stop him.

For the first time in my life, I heard Poppy stutter. A lawyer, who never asks a question unless he already halfway knows the answer, a smooth-voiced wordsmith, my grandfather looked at me and shook his head. "Justin." He stopped and started twice before he finally said the words.

"You need to know. Your father is . . . dressing and living as a woman named Christine right now." Poppy explained briefly where he'd found Dad, but his first sentence was all that kept ringing through my brain. *Dressing and living as a woman . . . Christine.*

While Poppy spoke, Ysabel looked at Mom, then at me, then back at Poppy. Grandmama looked at the table, trying to hold on to her composure. Eventually, Poppy's voice died, and he pressed his palms down on the table. We sat in silence.

After a long moment, Mom reached out a hand to Ysabel and the other to me. "Did you already know?" she asked. "Talk to me," she said, and her voice sounded ragged.

Ysabel swallowed. She looked at me, as if expecting me to jump in. I couldn't.

Mom's words were a rushed jumble, a little high-pitched. "I knew something was wrong. . . . I thought it was the job. Too much stress, maybe. Are you shocked? I've known for a little over a day, and it's still a shock to me. I still can't believe—no. Listen, I want us to count our blessings. Each of us is well and strong. We love each other. We will get through this."

Her positive voice shook so much at the end that it was hard to understand her words. Grandmama gave a little sob, and Poppy put his arm around her as she choked back her sadness. Mom gripped our hands, and Grandmama clung to Poppy, and we all just sat there. Ysabel, still clutching her stomach, had asked, "What do we do now?"

I still don't have an answer to that. I've tried to make lists of concerns and put together scenarios that make sense—*Dad becomes Christine, family becomes* . . . What? There are no answers.

I flip on my side and take a breath, rubbing my stomach where it feels like a ball of lava has taken up residence in my gut. Right after Poppy had talked to us, we'd taken the first steps toward dealing with things. Mom had told us Dad was staying up north in the little apartment he'd rented for his business trips. Poppy said that nothing was going to change right now, that Dad still was going to take care of things financially, and that we didn't have to worry.

Once Grandmama stopped crying, she said it wasn't the end of the world. I guess she was trying to comfort herself. She said that other children have transgender people for parents, that nobody's died of it. "We can all go on and survive this. All it takes is the right attitude," Grandmama said, and dragged out one of her usual sayings. *"This too shall pass."*

She may be right, but I can't imagine how. Nobody tells you how to get from the bad moment you're in to where you manage to live happily ever after.

I still don't know how I made the time pass, how I got through those first few days. Did it make me feel less alone to know that now Mom and Ysabel knew? Did it make me feel less crazy? All we did was put one foot in front of the other, go to school, go to work, come home, and exist. It wasn't enough, but it filled the moments. Until now.

I hold still and listen to Ysabel breathing. I slow my own breath, trying to match hers, feeling myself relaxing into drowsiness. Just when I'm on the edge of sleep, I'm back at school, standing at the podium, facing my opponents from Valley Jewish Day School, and Callista and her friend Geena in the front row. I'm letting them stew, making them wait for my final argument, when I'm distracted by a movement. I glance into the audience to see the woman in the white suit shifting, straightening her skirt. For some reason, Missy's comment about her being family distracts me. It's when she turns and looks over her shoulder that I see the resemblance; my father's profile is so clear that my knees start shaking. It's obviously Dad, in drag.

What. Is. Going. On.

If I can tell who he is, everyone will be able to when they see him. They can't see him. I can't let them look. There is a roaring in my ears as I step off the podium. Callista leans forward, her dark eyes fixed on me. She's watching me, so I don't look at him again; I can't. I step off the podium, and I fall and fall and—

Shut it down, Justin. Inhale, exhale. Just breathe.

I suck in air and wait for my heart to slow. The rest of that day had been hell. Mr. Lester had been shocked when I'd come to him with a drop slip for debate. "Justin, everybody chokes at least once. You have so much potential, so much promise that I really hate to see you do this. Are you sure you won't let me help you?"

"I'm sure, Mr. Lester. I'm just under too much stress. I can't do debate on top of everything else."

"You can always come back to the team," Mr. Lester had said, and I'd hated seeing the regret in his face. "You'll always be welcome."

Then later, it was my girlfriend's turn.

"Justin, I don't understand." Callista's nervousness showed in how she fiddled with the end of her braids. "What's going on? Why are you dropping out?"

"It's—look, Callista, I'm just going through some stuff, all right? I can't really talk about it."

Callista had clutched my arm. "Justin, please! I can keep a secret. It's not like I'm going to tell everyone what's going on. Just . . . talk to me!"

"I can't," I'd said, knowing I was throwing everything away and powerless to stop myself. "It's not you. It's me."

We had that conversation too many times to count. Sometimes crying, sometimes angry, Callista kept asking me to trust her.

She said she'd never give up on me, but she doesn't ask me to trust her anymore.

The whole school, it seemed, wanted to talk to me and ask what was wrong with me and why I'd thrown everything away. I dropped off of my social networking sites and stopped answering my phone, but there was no escape. Even Poppy told me he thought I was being selfish and letting everybody down. I almost told him what I'd seen then. But I didn't.

Why did I keep Dad's secret?

Dad knew I knew. Ysabel couldn't have cleaned up his stuff that well. The mug was pretty well smashed; it doesn't even hold water anymore, but Dad didn't ask us what had happened. He never said anything. It was as if this was all a crazy dream, that I'd imagined everything.

And that was the worst thing of all.

I kept thinking I'd screwed up, I'd seen it wrong. Maybe it was just somebody's mom. Maybe nothing happened at all. I kept praying that it was nothing, that it was just my imagination. It was all a nightmare, something that wormed into my brain and made things wrong. Dad could have made it right, if he'd just asked a question or said something. Instead, he said nothing, and I felt insane.

I must have finally fallen asleep, because I wake up with a little trickle of drool drying on the side of my face. *Ugh.* I wipe my mouth and sit up, trying to figure out what woke me in the first place. I hear another soft knock at the door a moment before it opens. Dressed in a pin-striped shirt and faded jeans, my father leans into the room.

"Ysabel—" he begins, then breaks off, a broad smile on his face. "Morning, Justin."

I rub my face and draw my knees to my chest. "Dad."

"You sleep okay down there?"

I shrug, hoping he'll get the message and go away, but he

only grins. "I remember when you and Ysabel turned six and got your own rooms. We found you like this every morning for months."

I just grunt. Dad's expression is amused. "Right. Well, breakfast is almost ready. You've got about an hour, but we're going to need to hustle. We have an appointment with the therapist this morning."

"What therapist?"

"Belly? Wake up now," Dad says, ignoring me.

"I said, 'What therapist?'" I repeat, my voice louder.

Dad raises his brows quizzically. "I told you we'd be seeing people this week, didn't I? Dr. Hoenig is a family therapist who specializes in transitioning families."

Panic claws at me, and it feels like my stomach drops through the floor. I cover the sick fear with anger. "Why do we have to go to the therapist when it's *your* problem? Why can't you go by yourself?"

Dad's eyebrows jerk, and I can see he's deciding what to say to that. He puts his hand on the doorknob and glances at his watch. "Fifty minutes now. Whether you have breakfast or not is up to you. Good morning, Ysabel." He pulls the door closed behind him with a decisive click.

Ysabel is sitting up, her bedhead hair a kinked and fuzzy frame for her tense face. "What's going on?"

I flop back onto the mattress, an arm in front of my eyes. "We're going to his therapist."

"A therapist?" I hear the mattress rustle as Ysabel moves. Her voice is closer. "Oh, okay, then. Good."

"What's 'good' about it?" I move my arm and glare up into her face. "Why should we have to listen to someone tell us all the

74

things we did to screw up Dad's life? I don't want to hear some crap about his bad childhood."

"You really think it'll be like that?" Ysabel stands and picks up her duffel bag. "Probably we're just going to talk to someone who's supposed to help us adjust or something."

"I don't want to talk to anyone." It's stupid, but her calmness is making me angrier. "I don't want help, and I don't want to adjust to anything."

Ysabel puts her bag on the bed and digs out a notebook and her Bible. "Yeah, well, life sucks, and then you find out no one cares what you want. You taking the first shower?"

"What are you doing with a journal? We don't have time for that."

Ysabel's mouth tightens. "Could you go somewhere else? Maybe to your *own* room? And mind your *own* business?"

I bounce up from the floor and drag my mattress toward the door. "Fine, whatever. It probably doesn't matter if we're late anyway."

"Would you shut up? I'm not going to make us late."

I open the door to my room, then pause. "Come get me before you go upstairs, okay?"

Ysabel's expression is mulish. "Why?"

"Because I'll wait for you. I'm not going up to stand around with Dad by myself."

"Like I had to last night."

I drag the mattress across the hall and throw it in the general direction of the box spring in my room. "Look, I'm sorry, okay? I fell asleep."

"Fine, whatever." Ysabel bends over her journal. "Close the door."

I dig through my bag for clean jeans and *The Constitution: I Read It for the Articles* T-shirt, and head into the bathroom, annoyed to see myself in the mirror, scowling. I've got to find my game face before we meet this therapist. This isn't going to be like the times when Mom dragged us to see Pastor Max, who only prayed with us and told us that we could just sit and listen to music or talk, if we wanted.

As I stand under the shower spray, I wonder what else is on my father's agenda. He mentioned outings and meeting trans-gender families. Is this what it's going to be like every time we come here? Does Dad seriously expect we're just going to fit in and hang out with these people? I feel another pulse of anger at Poppy and Grandmama. I still can't believe Poppy said they couldn't get involved. Why couldn't they have given us an out?

Breakfast is boxes of assorted cold cereals, fruit, yogurt, and bakery sweet rolls. Ysabel pours herself a bowl of some kind of granola clusters and eats it dry, like she always does, scanning the nutritional information on the side of the box, alternating each dry bite with a spoonful of yogurt.

Even annoyed with each other, we automatically double-team Dad. Despite his hovering, Ysabel and I drag out the meal as long as possible. Dad hates to be late even more than I do and finally insists that we have to leave *now*. Ysabel simply shrugs and carries her bowl of dry cereal with her. My father gives her an exasperated look, but doesn't say anything as he bundles us into the car and drives us downtown to a large suite of offices.

In the empty waiting room, which is a sickly mint green, we wait in silence, Dad standing relaxed by the door, Ysabel perched on a chair, reading a magazine, with her cereal balanced in her lap, and me, trying to pretend that all I'm doing is getting ready for a debate. The receptionist offers us coffee or tea, but I'm already wishing I hadn't eaten the roll I had for breakfast.

There's no clock in the waiting room, but I keep track of the minutes on my phone. I scroll through my email and see a notification from the Kids of Trans site; someone is requesting to chat with me off-line. I have begun to text a response when the door opens.

"Chris," the small gray-haired woman says happily, as if seeing Dad is the highlight of her day. "And these must be your twins."

I now realize why the waiting room is empty. There's a closed door on the other side of the doctor's office. The people she saw before us are already gone.

As the doctor and Dad exchange greetings, Ysabel stands, reaching into her bowl for a cereal cluster. She munches placidly as Dad introduces us.

"Guys, this is Dr. Hoenig. Dr. Hoenig, this is Ysabel, who is eldest by six minutes, and this is Justin."

"Nice to meet you both. Ysabel, I've got a spoon and some milk for that cereal if you'd like." Dr. Hoenig smiles.

"I'm good," Ysabel says, still maddeningly calm, following the woman into the office. "Thank you."

Dad glances back at me as I hesitate in the doorway. "Justin?"

It's only an hour, I remind myself. "Coming," I mutter.

"'Once more into the breach, dear friends.'" Dr. Hoenig smiles at me and gestures at the couch, love seat, and chairs set at angles to each other around a small rattan coffee table. "Sit anywhere, Justin. Let's get acquainted."

A Change of Script

Ysabel

At first it seems like the therapist isn't that bad. Dr. Hoenig is small and freckled and wrinkled like an apple doll, but her bright blue eyes and wide smile make her seem very young. Her slight accent, oversized red-framed glasses, and sleek gray bob remind me of the eccentric fashion designer Edna Mode in my favorite animated movie. I halfway expect her to try putting us in cape-free superhero costumes.

So far, Dr. Hoenig seems easygoing. She won't let Dad rush her to get started, and she hasn't let Justin's silent act throw her off. She even compliments me on my outfit—red hoodie, khaki cargo pants, and my rose-covered boots—which shows she's got style.

After a general chat, Dr. Hoenig moves on to the usual questions adults seem incapable of avoiding when talking to kids: what class we like best at school, what do we want to study in college, what are our plans for when we're done. Justin, who is Mr. Goals List and who came up with a comprehensive five-year plan when we were in the eighth grade, says "I don't know" in answer to her every question.

Dad's not taking that too well. Each time Justin opens his mouth, Dad shifts his shoulders against the back of his armchair, like he's forcing himself to stay in the seat. I glance at the clock above Dr. Hoenig's head, making a little bet with myself how long Dad will be able to keep his mouth shut.

"Do either of you have any idea where you want to attend college?" Dr. Hoenig asks.

"Penland or some craft school like it," I announce, and crunch another granola cluster.

"Justin?" Dr. Hoenig raises her eyebrows.

My brother shakes his head helplessly. "I don't know," he mutters, his eyes on the floor.

Dad's hand smacks against the arm of the chair and I glance at the clock to confirm. Yep. Sixty seconds.

"You 'don't know,' Justin?" my father bursts out.

"Chris?" Dr. Hoenig's bright blue eyes over her glasses are inquiring.

"I just can't believe he's going to sit there and lie to you," Dad sputters, shaking his head. "This boy was born knowing what he was going to do. I've never been as certain of anything in my whole life as—" My father breaks off and pinches the bridge of his nose, his eyes closed as he reins himself in. "Just answer the question, son."

"I did." Justin's voice is flat. "I don't know where I'm going to college."

"Stanford," Dad flashes back, his expression frustrated. "I've got the five-year plan on your wall practically memorized, just like everybody else in the family. Come *on*, Justin. It was a harmless, getting-to-know-you question. Would you just give this a chance?"

An elastic moment of silence stretches taut, and I tense, preparing for the inevitable, stinging snap as it breaks. My mouth dry, I stop fiddling with my cereal and pull my sleeves over my hands, waiting.

"Justin"—Dr. Hoenig's voice is kind but intent—"is there any reason you're not comfortable with talking about your future?"

I roll my eyes silently. Oh, man, here we go. Next she's going to ask him how he *feels* about his future.

"What about you, Ysabel? How do you feel about talking about your dreams and your future right now?"

At the word *feel*, a laugh slips out before I can control it. Dr. Hoenig just smiles at me calmly, but Dad's embarrassed expression piques my temper. What have *I* done that's so embarrassing? Irritated, I pick up another bit of cereal and scrutinize it before popping it into my mouth. I speak with my mouth full.

"Justin took down his five-year plan about six months ago, Dad. Just so you know."

Dad shoots a glance at me, then turns to face Justin. He leans forward, his elbows on his knees, and sighs deeply. "I didn't know that. I'm sorry." There's a pause. "So, you've changed your mind? About everything, Buddy?"

Justin shrugs, but his shoulders are so tight, it's more of a twitch. Dad hasn't really called him Buddy since he was ten. I wonder how Justin *feels* about that.

"It's kind of hard to be certain of your plans when so much else in your life has changed, isn't it?" Dr. Hoenig observes quietly.

Suddenly, it's not funny anymore. Justin exhales and looks up at Dr. Hoenig, misery in his expression.

"Yeah. It is."

We don't say much more that is important after that. Dr. Hoenig gives us this little sheet that says *Rights of Transgender Individuals* across the top. I scan it, and it's basically just human rights, so there are no surprises. Everyone has the right to feel good about themselves, wear what they want, and be loved, blah, blah, blah. That's obvious, and I get it, but then Dr. Hoenig says that she wants Justin and me to make up a list of our own rights . . . and talk about them with Dad.

Justin and I exchange a look, and I'm pretty sure he's as disgusted as I am. This definitely has the feel of a bogus make-work homework assignment. At least she didn't say we have to turn it back in to her or anything.

Dr. Hoenig is saying something else to Dad—probably giving him a bogus assignment, too—and I tune out for a minute, thinking. If it were me just doing this little Rights of Ysabel list for myself, I'd put down as number one that I have the right to expect my dad to be the same person I grew up with.

But according to the Transgender Person list . . . I don't have that right at all.

I shake my head, irritated. Does Dr. Hoenig seriously think we have any rights? Not only are we stuck doing whatever Dad wants us to do—not only because we're underage, but we're on his end of the state and we don't know anyone in this area—we can't force him to do anything. We can't make him stay Dad or make him go back to being the way he was. We can't make him give us back the world the way it was, and there is nothing on earth that can return me to the day before we found out that Dad was a transgender person. *Nothing*.

I close my eyes, breathing deeply to force the lid back on the volcano that opens up in me at these kinds of thoughts. We just need to be finished with this lady and do something else—anything else.

"What would you like to get out of your visit this week?" Dr. Hoenig is watching me closely, and I look away. "Justin? Chris? This is a question for all of you."

Dr. Hoenig waits as Dad answers, in detail of course. I really can't think of anything more than the usual spring break stuff—time to sleep in, time to try out some new glass techniques. Justin doesn't say much, either, but somehow this seems to make everyone worry. Dad and Dr. Hoenig spend the rest of our session trying to convince Justin to have some kind of goal for this week.

As if it matters.

Do any of them—Mom, Dad, or Dr. Hoenig—think Justin and I have failed to notice how little control we have over any of this? No matter how many imaginary goals we might have, the thing is, it's all decided. By her actions and his response, Mom and Dad have essentially figured out between the two of them how the rest of our lives will go, at least until we leave home.

So, what's the point?

"I think we've made a good start today," Dr. Hoenig says, looking up at Dad as we stand on the landing in front of her back door. "Take care, Nicholas family."

"We'll see you tomorrow," Dad says, and my jaw drops.

"We're not doing this every day, are we?" I ask. Dad and Dr. Hoenig just smile, Dr. Hoenig with sympathy, and then we're out the door and down the stairs.

Justin manages to be out in front, jogging down the stairs while Dad holds me to a more leisurely pace.

"This hasn't been that bad, has it, Belly?" Dad asks over his shoulder.

"Don't call me that." I clutch my bowl and glare at him.

"Sorry," Dad says, raising his hands defensively. "Habit, Ysabel."

I give him a disgusted look and push past him down the stairs.

My father takes his sweet time getting to the car, twirling his keys around his finger. Justin and I are waiting impatiently for him as he uses the remote, which unlocks the doors with a subdued click.

"Well, gang, it's a little bit early for lunch"—Dad raises his voice as he climbs into the front seat—"but I thought we could take in a matinee or something. Unless anyone else has a suggestion?"

"Seriously?" I glance at Justin. Dad's never taken us to a matinee; he's more of a DVD-at-home type of guy, mainly because he's too cheap to spring for theater popcorn, and he talks to the characters on-screen, as if they can hear him.

"There's nothing good out." Justin shrugs and puts on his seat belt.

"That doesn't matter," I widen my eyes in a pointed stare at my brother, simply eager not to return to Dad's silent, sterile apartment. "Do we get popcorn?"

My father chuckles. "Yes, Ysabel, you can have your popcorn, but save some room; we're going to a Mexican grill for lunch, because God knows, the two of you need to eat some vegetables after last night." He puts the key in the ignition. "Or there's The Raven, a little independent theater that sometimes shows double features of old monster flicks. Shall we see if they're open?"

"Why do you want to go to the movies?" Justin asks, crossing his arms.

My father leans back against the driver's seat and sighs. "Honestly, Justin? Because right now, sitting in a dark room is about all I'm good for."

My brother shrugs and looks out the window.

"Hey"—Dad leans around the driver's seat again—"that was a joke, Buddy. This movie thing is just one option. If you'd rather we went somewhere and talked, we can do that."

I make an exasperated noise. "You can drop me off at the movies if you do," I warn him. "I'm through talking." I turn and glare at my brother.

Justin looks at me, anger and guilt and apology in his expression. "I'm sorry, but a movie just seems like a waste of time," he says tightly. He turns to Dad. "I mean, isn't there supposed to be some point to this? What are we supposed to be doing here? What is seeing a therapist supposed to accomplish? Is that why you aren't wearing a dress?"

I suck in a quiet breath, not sure if I'm scared or glad Justin doesn't believe in subtle.

Dad smiles a little. "No, Justin, I'm sorry to disappoint you; it's not about Dr. Hoenig. I'm not wearing a dress because I don't want to right now."

Justin makes a disbelieving noise, and my father rubs his face and sighs.

"Okay, Justin. Look—first, this is your vacation—I haven't forgotten that. I want us to have some fun. Second, we're meeting with Dr. Hoenig in the hopes that she'll make it easier for all of us to say the things to each other that we need to say. Finally— I repeat—I am not wearing a dress because I don't want to at the moment. This week is about you and Ysabel. I care more about your comfort than my wardrobe. Are we clear?"

Justin looks away again, bouncing his knee. "Fine."

"So, can I get my popcorn, or can you give it a rest yet?" I ask, somehow angry that Justin has managed to be up front with Dad without sounding like a jerk and I have not.

Justin gives me an odd look. "What's your problem?"

"Low blood sugar, probably." Dad puts the car in gear and pulls out of the parking slot. "Let's just get an early lunch. None of us ate enough for breakfast, and The Cantina has some great fajitas."

"There's nothing wrong with my blood sugar," I sputter. "And I'm a vegetarian, hello. I don't want fajitas."

"They have asparagus and mushroom fajitas, too," Dad says mildly. "We'll have a good lunch and talk some more. Justin's right—we don't have a lot of time."

Justin's right, I mimic savagely to myself. Of course he is. I cross my arms and slide down in the seat, feeling baffled and frustrated. I don't mind getting fajitas—the idea of some real food after gorging on junk food last night is a good one—but it seems like somehow Justin has managed to come off as seriously concerned about Dad and our family issues, and I've come off as . . . the snarky girl with the low blood sugar who's shallow and all about popcorn.

I glance at Justin's profile as he stares out the window and make up my mind. He's not the only one who can ask direct questions. If Dad wants to have a talk, we'll *talk*.

Happy Meal

Justin

JustC: GAH! sick. of. talking.
Styx: hear that.
C4Buzz: Silence is golden but duct tape is silver.
JustC: lol

I expect fake cacti and piñatas at a Mexican grill, neither of which The Cantina has. This place is white tablecloths and valet parking nice—far too nice for just a middle-of-the-day lunch with Dad. Even Ysabel's looking around with interest, checking out the painted floor tiles, pottery, and lantern-looking metal light fixtures, probably so she can steal the designs and make them for her next art project.

The waitress leaves each of us a leather folder containing the menu and points out the specials with a smile. Dad nods to her and absorbs himself in choosing a meal.

Guitar music underscores the quiet conversation around us. Everything is so classy and understated, from the lighting to the menu to the chime of forks on plates, that all the mature-sounding conversation I'd planned gets stuck in my throat. When Ysabel sits forward and breaks the silence, I'm relieved.

"Did you bring us someplace this fancy so we won't actually say anything?"

I want to laugh at my father's startled expression.

"Will it work?" His voice is dry.

"No." Ysabel leans back in her seat. "I just wondered."

"You have to admit, this place is pretty classy," I point out. "I thought we were just going to a taqueria or something."

Dad shrugs. "I thought this conversation deserved a good setting."

I wish the setting would actually make a difference to what he has to say.

Dad orders a *salsa de aguacate* for all of us, which comes with our iced tea and baskets of tortilla chips. The restaurant is filling quickly, and the noise level is rising, which gives me courage. But before I can open my mouth, Ysabel takes a deep breath and turns to Dad.

"Okay." She clears her throat. "I've been looking on the Internet, and I have some questions."

I blink and sit back. *Go, Ys.*

"All right." Dad looks at Ysabel seriously. "Do you understand that I might not be able to answer everything?"

"Why not?" I challenge him.

Dad looks at me. "Because . . . some things don't have answers. Because some things I don't know. Because everyone is different, and I can only answer for me. Because . . . I'm still your dad, and as a parent, I don't have to tell my children things they don't need to know. Just . . . because." He shrugs a little helplessly. "I don't mean to disappoint you. You have the right to ask me any question and I reserve the right to hear the question and not answer."

"You sound like a lawyer," Ysabel accuses, and I agree with a dissatisfied grunt.

"Well, my father-in-law is one of the best." Dad smiles briefly. "Let's hear it."

Ysabel fiddles with her sleeves, not meeting Dad's eyes. "When was the first time you wanted to dress in . . . to wear . . ." Ysabel trails off, clears her throat, and tries again. "When did you first want to dress up?"

There's a heartbeat of stillness. Dad moves his water glass, then fiddles absently with his napkin. "My whole life," he says finally.

My mouth opens before I can stop the words. "Your whole *life?*" I blurt. "You *knew* you were like this?"

Dad looks down at his glass of water and deliberately reaches for it, making a ceremony out of grasping the straight cylinder, touching it to his lips, and setting it back on the table. "When I was four," he says carefully, using his long fingers to line up the napkin with the edge of the table, "I was in a cousin's wedding. I was the Bible boy. I remember being so jealous that my cousin Lily got to wear a dress with little white beads and lace, and a tiara with sequins. She got to be the flower girl, and all I got was a black suit. No tiara." He looks up and smiles crookedly. "That used to be one of my great-aunt Wilma's favorite stories about me, about how I fell on the floor at the rehearsal dinner in a screaming fit, because Lily wouldn't let me wear her tiara. My folks were still alive, back then."

Dad doesn't talk much about his parents or the great-aunt who raised him after their deaths in a car crash when he was eight, so it's hard to break the silence that follows.

Ysabel's voice, when it comes, is tentative. "So, you knew when you were four you wanted a tiara, but when did you start really dressing up?"

"In college." Dad chews his bottom lip and doesn't elaborate. I get the feeling there's more he could say and wonder if I asked, if this is one of the questions he would refuse to answer.

I pile chips onto my appetizer plate, aware of a nervous energy that I need to burn, even though I'm not sure I have much of an appetite left. I've already had enough of this conversation, but we can't stop when we've just gotten started, and there's something I have to ask. I busy myself ladling salsa on my chips.

"So, you're not gay." It's a statement, but somehow my voice still sounds uncertain.

Dad watches me patiently. "No."

"And you're not going to . . . be gay. I mean, you're not going to"—my gesture is vague, my eyes stray to a spot above his head—"have a surgery."

Dad shakes his head and fidgets with his glass again. "Surgery wouldn't make me gay. Wearing women's clothes doesn't make me gay. I'm not sexually interested in *men*." He looks up steadily. "Either way, surgery's not an option for me."

"Why?" Ysabel blurts, and Dad grimaces and rubs his forehead.

"It's not something I need," he says awkwardly. He shifts back in his seat, the fake leather squeaking a little under his worn jeans, and unbuttons his cuffs to roll up his sleeves. "Ys, I'm not sure I can explain that one to you, any more than I can explain the reasons behind wanting to wear women's clothes." Dad lowers his voice, flicking a quick glance around the room. I can't help but follow suit, staring at the profiles of the people at the tables around us. They're having business conversations or laughing and smiling with friends. Only we look tense.

Dad's shoulders hunch as he scoots his chair forward. He clears his throat and reaches for the basket of chips closest to him. I can see the shine of sweat along his hairline. "Anything else?"

"Yes," Ysabel says, taking control of the conversation again. "Did you know anyone else like you? I mean, in your family?"

"It's not genetic," my father says, his gaze flicking to meet mine. I flinch and feel my face get hot. "Being transgender is not something you can inherit or catch."

"I know that," I mutter, feeling both insulted and relieved.

"To answer the question," Dad says, turning to my sister with a slight smile, "no. I never met another adult male in my family who dressed in any nontraditional way. I didn't meet any males who dressed nontraditionally, period, until I was in college. A bunch of us went to the city to hear a comedian. He was a female impersonator, and there were a lot of transsexual people in the club. It was . . . quite an experience."

I move my shoulders uncomfortably, weirded out by the thoughtful tone in my father's voice. I decide I don't want to know what "quite an experience" means.

"So, how'd you learn to wear makeup?" Ysabel asks. Mouth open, I turn my head and stare at her. How is she coming up with this stuff? She must have been thinking of all these questions for days, while all I've been doing is trying *not* to think.

"Kind of trial and error," Dad admits, and shrugs, fingering the edge of his water glass. "I visited a lot of how-to sites on the Internet. I bought a lot of makeup by mail order." He smiles, the corners of his eyes crinkling. "It's a work in progress."

"Did you wear Mom's makeup?" I hear the accusation in my voice.

Dad shakes his head immediately. "No. That's hers. I have my own."

I shift my weight, feeling sweat prickling in my armpits. I wish he wouldn't say crap like that. Every time I start to feel like we're just here, being with Dad, in a restaurant, he keeps reminding me that this whole conversation is crazy, and that he's . . . changed.

Ysabel clears her throat. "All right. Moving on," she continues doggedly, smoothing her hair behind her ears. "Is Christine a different person, or is she . . . you." Ysabel looks up.

"Well." Dad chews his bottom lip, and I realize I am doing the same thing. I stop and wipe my mouth with the back of my hand. "Christine is, let's say, an aspect of me. She's both me and more than me. How's that for confusing?" He smiles.

"So basically you've got a split personality," I say.

Dad barks out a laugh. "You might look at it that way," he says. "You'd be wrong, but you might look at it that way."

"Well, what's right, then?" Ysabel asks, a little braver because Dad seems so unbothered by the question. "I mean, we have *no* idea, Dad. You laugh, but as far as we knew eight months ago, you were just Christopher Nicholas, one guy. Now there's almost . . . two of you."

My father sobers immediately. "I know. I'm sorry. I don't mean to make light of this, Belly. It's just that I've had the same questions myself along the way. It's hard to think of yourself as sane when you feel like you're two people. When I'm Christine, I am all of who I am. When I'm Christopher, I'm only . . . half of who I should be." He says the words with conviction.

"So, Christine is more than half of you." My smile is twisted. "Which half of you is in love with Mom?"

"Good question." Ysabel is blinking hard, and her arms are wrapped around her abdomen again. "That's what I want to know."

Dad looks visibly startled, though he tries to hide it. "Justin. Belly." There's a tenderness in his voice that makes my stomach hurt. He reaches across the table to grab my sister's hand.

"I said not to call me that." Ysabel leans out of reach. "Answer the question, Dad. Which one of you is married? Which one of you fell in love with Mom? Which one of you has been with her all this time? Christine can't be married to Mom."

My father rubs the heel of his hand across his forehead and looks uncomfortable. "Guys, that's . . . I love your mother. That's what I can tell you. Aside from that, questions about your mom and me are between Mom and me."

"That's a cop-out. It's not a personal question," I object.

"Actually, it's—"

"No. If you're only half of who you are when you're our father, are you saying you weren't married to Mom the whole way?" I put down my fork and wrap my arms around my aching middle. "So, does that mean Christine can have a relationship with someone else who could be with *all* of her? Is that how it goes?"

"Justin." My father's voice is thick with hurt. His mouth firms into a line, and he just stares at me for a moment, his expression caught between disbelief and frustration. "You know me better than that. You know I would never hurt your mother like that, never. *Never.*"

"We know you 'better than that'?" Ysabel's voice is disbelieving. "Are you serious? Dad, *who* do I know? Half the time you're this more-than-Christopher *Christine*. Eight months ago, I didn't even know there *was* a Christine. What makes you think we know you at all?"

"Ysabel, honey, you're making this way too complicated," Dad says, and rubs a hand over his face. He gestures, holding out his hands, trying to bridge the distance between us. "I know it's tough to understand, but I'm part of Christine. Christine is still me. You know me. You know who I am."

"No, we don't." Ysabel and I say the words together, and she shoots a glance at me. I nod. It feels stupid to say to Dad, a man we've known all our lives, but it's true. If he's Christine, we have no idea who he is.

"*Sopa* Azteca, *señor?*" our waitress chirps. A sizzling sound and billows of fragrant steam suddenly envelop our table. Dad nods, looking dazed, as she sets the large bowl of tortilla soup in front of him. The kitchen lackeys following her present Dad's chipotle enchilada, my taco platter, and Ysabel's veggie fajitas. All the while she's explaining what's what and setting down the sides and the other waitstaff are refilling our iced tea and bringing more chips, we all just sit there, silent. Ysabel stares fixedly at the tablecloth. My father smiles vaguely at the waitress, leaning

93

away from the table so she can bustle around him, but there's a stiffness to his face. The slope of his shoulders telegraphs hurt, and I look down at my plate, wishing I was hungry, wishing that we were just all here for real, being together like before.

But Ysabel has it right—we're here to say something to each other. And as the waitress bustles away, I decide there's no time like the present.

"We don't know you, Dad," I repeat quietly, looking up at him. "No offense, but . . . I don't want to know, either. Not . . . the Christine part." I shrug. "I'm sorry, but . . . it's how I feel."

My father tries to smile, but the attempt falls short. His mouth twitches. "Well, that was the risk, wasn't it?" he says finally, his voice threaded with weariness. "I had hoped that you would never . . . that we would never be . . ." He stops, and everything hangs, for a moment, in that silence, which goes on forever. I shift my feet and pick up my fork, drawing away a piece of shredded lettuce from my taco and chasing it around my plate. Dad finally clears his throat. I look up at him, and there is kindness and tiredness and grief in his eyes. "I hope you both get a chance to get to know me again."

I look away. Dad wants me to understand this and be okay with things, but I can't. I can't understand this . . . thing he's doing. I don't want to lose my father in a trade for someone named Christine, but he's already gone. I don't know how to take that, or what to do. I don't know how to deal with this Christine person he's left behind.

I just want my dad back.

Many Waters

Ysabel

Dad pulls into the garage and shuts off the engine. Justin and I climb out silently, and Justin carefully lifts the paper bag filled with our lunch from where it sat on the floor between his feet.

Unlocking the back door, my father goes inside and drops his keys on the hook next to the door. He pauses in the living room as I turn toward the stairs, and Justin heads for the kitchen to put away the food.

"I appreciated your thoughts today," Dad says awkwardly. Justin gives a little cough and pauses at the counter. I take a step down into the stairwell, unsure what, if anything, I should say.

"This conversation isn't over," Dad continues, making eye contact with both of us. "We can take a break right now and have some downtime, or we can keep on."

"Break," Justin blurts. "I need to—I'm going downstairs."

Dad looks at me. "Ysabel?"

"Break," I agree heavily. Despite the fact that it's early afternoon, I'm exhausted.

"All right." Dad nods. "I think I'm going to drive out to the reservoir for a run, then I'll come home and we'll try and eat lunch again." He smiles wryly. "Can't let my fancy enchiladas go to waste."

I nod and start down the stairs again. I have free time now and could set up some torchwork, or at least twist some of the copper wire I brought for earrings. But something about both the trip to Dr. Hoenig's and the conversation over lunch has burned out any creative juices I had.

"Justin?" Dad's invitation is tentative. "Want to go for a run with me? The reservoir is beautiful—it's a four-mile loop through parkland and trees. Some long hills, but nothing you can't handle."

"Uh, no. Thanks," Justin says, and I hear the fridge door close.

"Maybe next time," Dad says. A moment later, his bedroom door closes.

I pause in the stairwell, waiting for my brother. He comes down the stairs, his face slack with weariness. He looks unsurprised to find me waiting. "I really need a break, Ysabel," he warns, pushing past me.

"I know," I say, following him down. I follow him to his room and barely stop him from closing the door in my face. "Wait. Can I have five minutes?"

"Fine." Justin kicks his mattress until it aligns with his box spring, then flops down on his back, his arm flung across his face.

I stand in the doorway, watching him, then cross and sit on the edge of the bed, scooting back a little until my hip touches his leg. "So, you're going to sleep for a while?"

"Maybe." Justin's voice is a thread. "I need to shut down."

I understand how he feels. "Me too," I say. "I only wanted to be sure you're okay."

"I'm fine," Justin rubs his face. "I just can't talk anymore." He rolls to his side, his back to me.

I lean my forehead on his shoulder. "That's okay. We don't have to," I say. I reach around him and find his hand, grasping his clenched fist until his fingers grip mine. We huddle, walled in by our own sadness, together, but on our own.

What if we never get over this? All I can imagine is this loss infecting our happiness for years and years, like an abscess, and nothing making the pain lessen.

I love Dad—more than anything. But right now, I would give anything to make this bad feeling go away.

The crook in my neck wakes me, and I realize I am still in Justin's room, sprawled awkwardly on the edge of his bed, my arm slung around his shoulders. I straighten stiffly, carefully getting to my feet so I don't wake him.

The house is still. I walk up the stairs to the front entryway and crack open the door to the garage. No car. The clock on the microwave says it's almost four, and for a moment, I feel a twinge

97

of worry. Dad said his run was only four miles. How far away is this reservoir? What if something happened to him?

A note on the fridge makes me breathe a sigh of relief. *Picking up some stuff for breakfast tomorrow. Back in an hour.* —Dad

I wander into the living room and look at the deck, which is now in the shade of the huge live oak tree next to it. I consider setting up my kiln on the table there, but the idea of getting out my case just makes me tired. Instead, I settle for the brain-dead activity of the hour and search the living room for the TV remote.

As usual, there's nothing decent to watch at this time of day. I stretch out on the couch and consider going back to sleep, but quickly get bored with trying to think restful thoughts. I wander through the tiny dining room, fiddling with the pillow on Dad's armchair, stacking up the coasters, and peering at the watercolors in their plain black frames. I open the drawers beneath the television cabinet and find them empty except for a whisper of dust. Finding myself in front of Dad's bedroom door, I take a deep breath and turn the knob.

It's locked.

I blink, shocked, and twist the knob one way and then the other. Mom and Dad's door is *never* locked. None of us ever lock our bedroom doors at home. Baffled, I find myself rattling the knob again and stop, slowly releasing the smooth metal sphere. Obviously, things are different now. This isn't Mom *and* Dad's door; in this place, it's Dad's door. And Dad has something to hide.

I back away to look for my father in his bland beige house. I snoop through the kitchen, opening every cabinet and all of the drawers, counting the silverware and the place settings. In the drawer beneath the phone, I find a phone book, a pad and pen, a few packets of breath mints, stray rubber bands, and all the mundane detritus of Dad's austere life. I also see a yellow-handled screwdriver.

The idea strikes like lightning, and I'm across the room almost before I can think it through. I want to find out who Dad's become. It's not like I'm looking for something bad; I only want to know. I ignore the whisper in my head, warning me to slow down and think. I want to know something more about Christopher Nicholas, something he can't filter or decide not to tell. I want to know as much about him as he is holding back.

There are only two cross-marked screws, and they're tighter than I expected. Probably no one has taken the knob off of this door before. But it's five minutes' work, sweating and slipping and nicking my thumb, then my fingers are pressed against the rough hole where the handle once was, and I'm pushing open the door, and—

The air crowds my throat with tears, and I stand in the doorway to my father's room, staggering under the weight of memory, feeling my chest squeeze.

It smells like him. Like his safe Dad smell of a citrusy cologne, the moisturizer Mom makes him use, his shampoo, and the ink from the pen he always carries in his jacket pocket, all concentrated into one place. The smell of coffee and wood and drafting lead, the smell of security and familiarity and routine. This room smells like home, like everything I've been missing for so long.

This is the only room in the whole house that looks right. The pillows on the king-sized bed and the matching duvet are a deep navy, just like Mom and Dad's at home. Though the bed is mostly made, the pillows are stacked haphazardly, and there are two alarm clocks, one on each night table. I wrap my arms around myself, staring. Did he lie? Is someone else sleeping with Dad?

I barely take in the rest of the items on the night table—on the right, a box of tissues, Dad's open Bible, and a notebook, closed. On the left, a desk lamp, a tidy stack of newspapers, and engineering journals. Beneath the window is a glass-topped counter that holds Dad's computer and a blueprint. At the foot of the bed, there's a dresser and a bookshelf, with a picture of Justin and me when we graduated from the eighth grade and another of all of us on our last vacation in Colorado.

I pick up the heavy silver frame and study my father's high cheekbones, his long, straight nose, wide mouth, and crooked smile. Mom says in college Dad looked like a dark-skinned Harry Connick Jr., all awkward long arms and big hands. She'd thought he was geeky until she'd seen him smile. She'd fallen in love with his dimples.

I stare at the picture, trying to find a resemblance to the jazz musician. Instead, I see an echo of my own sharp nose and wide eyes. I set the picture down, straightening it so it looks as if it hasn't moved.

I brush my fingers over the pages of Dad's Bible, then hesitate over the notebook beneath.

We always would see Dad writing things. He'd take a note-book to church and write. Sometimes in the summer he'd sit in the backyard and write in the morning while he was drinking his coffee. I was never really curious about it. After all, Justin and I had our own notebooks. Dad said his notebook wasn't his diary; it was just full of things he was thinking about, things he wrote down so he could think them through clearly.

My fingers itch to open the thin cardboard cover and see what my father has written on those neat blue lines. I want a clue to his thoughts—I want to know what's in his mind now, where we'll all end up. I want to know if he's been alone in this bed. But as I reach for it, my conscience stings, and my hand drops.

I haven't really done anything wrong yet, not too wrong, really. But I know I cannot open that notebook. There is a line from curiosity to invasion that I just can't cross.

Sighing, I clench my inquisitive fingers and walk around the rest of the room. Dad's bathroom door is open, and moist towels—only one set—hang on the shower stall. I tiptoe into the tiny space that houses the toilet and open the mirrored cabinets above the sink. One is empty, the other holds aspirin and cough medicine. The walk-in closet across from the sink area is illuminated by the warm lights above the mirror, and I move toward it instinctively, my hand brushing the wool fabric of slacks and jacket. I look up and see Dad's hard hat on a shelf, the name of his company on the front. I push deeper, looking for secrets and answers. Does Dad have the Christine dresses in here? What if he has wigs?

My heart freezes as my fingers encounter something silky. When I can force myself to look, I see it's just Dad's luau shirt, the bright short-sleeved, floral-printed one Mom bought him for our church beach party, but it's enough to scare me into backing out of the closet, my pulse thudding a panicked tempo in my throat.

I lean against the wall to catch my breath, my gasps quick and shallow. I realize I don't want to know about my father's other life. I don't want to see him as Christine. I don't want evidence that everything's changed.

I don't really want to know him.

"So, why are you in here, stupid?" I mutter to myself. I turn toward the door and find my glance captured once again by the notebook. I hesitate, knowing I don't want to know what's in there. Still, the fear pulls me away as strongly as the desperate curiosity urges me forward.

I step closer, lifting the Bible and disturbing the pages. A worn blue envelope slides from between the pages and falls. I bend and pick it up, my eyes widening. It's addressed to Christine Nicholas.

He said he would never hurt Mom. He said I knew him better than that.

My heart pounding, I slip the pretty notepaper from the envelope, breathing in the faint perfume as I unfold it. I suck in air as I recognize my mother's careful, precise script, and my eyes follow the lines:

Set me as a seal upon your heart, as a seal upon your arm,
for love is stronger than death, and jealousy as cold as the
grave; its flames burn with a mighty fire like the fires of hell.
But many waters cannot quench love, and floods cannot
drown it. If one were to give all the wealth of his house for
love, his riches would be utterly condemned.

The words are faintly familiar, and I realize they're from the Bible. Beneath the verse, she has written just the word

Always.

Hastily, I refold the letter, fingers clumsy. What am I *doing?* I shouldn't be here. I have trespassed into something hugely private between my parents, and I'm embarrassed—oh Lord, so embarrassed—and irritated with myself. If Dad ever read my journal or broke into my room, I'd never stop screaming about it. This was a horrible idea.

And yet, as I lean against Dad's open door, hurriedly fitting the screws back into the knob, I feel a strange center of calm. How can they be getting a divorce? Mom and Dad, in spite of this Christine thing, are somehow still in love.

I refuse to hope for anything, but even as I try to smother it, a tiny spark remains.

I drop the screwdriver and fumble after the last screw, feeling around blindly in the carpet under Dad's desk. Scowling, I grab the knob and rattle it. Even without the last screw, it looks like it will stay in place, and if I can—

It's only a whisper of air over my skin, but all of my muscles tense. Dry-mouthed, I push to my feet as the garage door clicks shut. I meet my father's sharp gaze as he walks down the stairs from the entryway, watch the understanding bloom on his face as he looks from the screwdriver in my hands to the evidence of the open door behind me. And then his eyes narrow in an expression of pure fury.

"*Get. Out.*"

Moving through the doorway as far from his visibly shaking body as I can, I drop the screwdriver and run.

The Hardest Word

Justin

Stretching, I yawn and squint at the small screen on my phone.

There are currently 3 Guests and 5 Users online
at Kids of Trans Forum Chat.
Online Users:
C4Buzz
Viking
Amberheart
Styx

Leary
JustC

C4Buzz: Are people just lurking, cuz no one is
saying anything?
JustC: Yeah . . . it says Styx is on, but s/he
hasn't posted anything . . . huh.
Viking: So, what's going on with you?
JustC: Still here in boo-cannon. Sick of it.
C4Buzz: That's your dad's, right? not going
good?
Viking: Buchannan? Rlly? Live near there.
JustC: It's okay . . . just . . . a little real, u kno?
Was easier at home.
C4Buzz: Yeah. Easier to keep your head
straight.
Viking: JustC, g2g. Message me norseman@
animail.net if u want to get togethr. Bye

A quick knock. Before I can say anything, the door opens
and Ysabel hurtles in. Her eyes are wide, and she's blinking hard.
She closes the door silently and slides to the floor behind it.

"What happened?" I ask, halfway sitting up.

"Nothing," Ysabel says, and draws her knees to her chest.
She's shaking.

"Don't give me that. Ys?"

"I don't want to talk about it."

Okay, then. I wait, but she won't look at me. After a moment,
I lie back and look at my phone screen again.

Amberheart: Ezr when u don't have 2 c.

C4Buzz: Hey Amberheart. Bad day?

Amberheart: No. Talkng 2 JustC.

JustC: ???

Amberheart: Ez 2 freak when u c the clothes.

JustC: Didn't see clothes.

Amberheart: Huh.

JustC: No x-dress. Just trying 2 deal—

"Justin?" Dad calls, and knocks. Ysabel scoots into the corner behind the door.

JustC: g2g. Bye.

I tuck my phone out of sight and sit up. "Yeah?"

My father opens the door and steps in, holding up the cordless phone. "Mom wants to say hello. And then give the phone to your sister."

I take the phone, shooting a glance at Ysabel, who is sitting hunched in on herself, her head down. Dad backs out of the room and closes the door behind him without even looking in her direction. Frowning, I put the phone to my ear.

"Mom?"

"Hey, Justin." My mother's voice is warm. "How's it going?"

"It's okay, I guess."

"Are you sleeping all right? Did you remember your mouth guard?"

I roll my eyes, glad she can't see me. "Yeah, I'm sleeping okay so far. You cooking anything interesting?"

Mom makes a so-so noise. "Just a company brunch, nothing too interesting."

"Oh." Silence hums along the phone lines.

"Well, I guess you guys are going rafting tomorrow, huh?" my mother continues brightly.

"We're *what?*"

"Oops. I hope that wasn't supposed to be a surprise."

"What does Dad know about rafting?"

Mom laughs. "Probably more than you do," she says. "You're going with a group, though."

"Oh." Belatedly I remember that Dad said he wanted to introduce us to other transgender people and their families. "I guess it's better meeting them outside than sitting through one more therapy thing. Although Dr. Hoenig is all right," I add quickly.

"That's good. I'm glad you like her."

There's another pause as I try and figure out what Mom called to hear. She knows I'm okay. She knows I'm getting along with Dad all right. I shrug, at a loss. "So, did you want something else, or do you want to talk to Ys?"

"I see your phone manners haven't improved." Mom gives a long-suffering sigh. "If you can tear yourself away, I'd like you to call me tomorrow when you're home from rafting, all right? I love you. Now let me talk to Ysabel."

"Love you, bye," I reply, and hand over the phone.

I flop back on the bed as Ysabel says hello and consider another nap. It's quiet in the room for a long, long time. I've almost forgotten Ysabel's on the phone when she suddenly begins her one-sided conversation.

"I know. I know. I know. Mom, I'm sorry. I know. I just . . . I didn't mean—"

I roll up on my elbow, frowning. Ysabel might have been caught eavesdropping again. Last time, Mom lectured her for days about it, and she lost her privileges to take some class or other at The Crucible, which to her was a big, big deal. Grand-mama still lectures her about it, too, which is worse than any punishment.

"No. I know. I know I do. No, Mom, I can't. Well, yeah, but I can't—" Ysabel listens some more and swipes her sleeve across her nose. She's crying. Seriously worried, I sit up.

"I know, Mom. I'm sorry," she repeats, her voice wobbly. "I love you, too. Bye."

Ysabel tosses the phone to me and drops her forehead to her knees.

"Are you going to tell me, or am I supposed to pretend you're not crying?"

Ysabel glares at me, her eyes slightly watery and red. "I broke into Dad's room, okay? And he caught me."

I blink. "Okay, wait—what?"

"It was locked." Ysabel swallows hard. "I found a screwdriver."

"Oh, crap. Did you—" I stop the words. I shouldn't ask her what she saw.

Ysabel rubs her face. "I don't even know what I was looking for. I just wanted to know why he'd locked the door."

I nod. "I can see that."

"Well, you're the only one," Ysabel sighs. "I either have to talk about it with Dad and 'make a meaningful restitution'"—she makes air quotes—"or withdraw from the Phoenix Fire Festival."

My mouth drops. Everyone who knows my sister knows how

much the Fire Festival and The Crucible mean to her. "Wow. If Mom's threatened the Fire Festival, you know she's deadly serious. You'd better apologize fast."

Ysabel turns miserable eyes on me. "I can't. What am I supposed to say? 'I'm sorry about the breaking and entering; I didn't mean anything by it'?"

I wince. "Well, 'I'm sorry' seems a pretty obvious place to start."

"He already knows I'm sorry," she mutters.

"Yeah, well, you get extra points on the restitution scale if you say it out loud," I remind her. "Trust me, I know what to do, since usually I'm the one who argues with him and pisses him off. Just say you're sorry and agree with whatever he says, or you'll be there forever."

Ysabel hunches over again. "He won't accept my apology. This isn't like snooping for Christmas presents when we were little, Justin. You should have seen him. He was so far beyond pissed. He could barely talk."

I rub my arms, imagining. "I guess you can always do the Festival next year, right?"

"No!" Ysabel slaps her palms against the floor, glaring at me. "The Crucible is all I have left. I'm sorry I was stupid and broke into Dad's room, but it's not fair to take away my show. It's got nothing to do with Dad!"

"Shooting the messenger," I warn her, leaning back from her intensity. "I'm not the one you're mad at, Ys."

"None of you understand," Ysabel rages, struggling to her feet. "Nobody made you give up debate, Justin. You walked away. The Crucible is the only place I fit, and they're not taking it from me!"

Ysabel storms out of my room and slams the door. A second later, I hear another slam from across the hall.

I exhale a long breath and get up. Ysabel has completely blown all thoughts of a nap out of me, and remembering Dad's comment before lunch about her blood sugar, I decide to get something to eat.

Scooping up the phone, I wander upstairs and chuck it on the kitchen counter. Dad's door is closed, and there's no sign of life from either him or Ysabel. I shrug and bring my takeout tray and plastic fork into the living room. I watch TV while I demolish my four tacos and wonder how mad Ys will be if I eat her little side of beans and rice.

Not too mad, I decide, and polish them off.

Unexpectedly, Dad's door opens as I'm throwing away my foam tray and rinsing my plastic fork. He wanders into the kitchen in a familiar pair of gray sweats and a ratty Chi Epsilon T-shirt.

"Hey, Buddy." He takes Ysabel's takeout tray and tucks it in the microwave.

"Hey, Dad," I reply cautiously. He looks more tired than angry.

"I've got ice cream, if you want any." Dad pulls a plastic bag out of the freezer.

I ignore the small pints of fudge brownie, chocolate chunk, and caramel ripple in favor of the larger container of vanilla bean. "Did you get root beer?"

Dad smirks and opens the refrigerator to pull out a liter of my favorite. "Of course. I still know how to do that much."

"Just checking," I say.

The microwave beeps. Dad gingerly removes Ysabel's takeout

tray and puts it on the counter. "I'll tell you what," he says, opening the cabinet and pulling out two tall glasses. "You go ahead and take your sister her dinner, and I'll make us floats. All right?"

I grab a pile of napkins from the counter and the bag with Ysabel's tortillas and the rest of her sides. "Sounds good," I say.

I kick Ysabel's door, and she opens it right away, a wary expression on her face. She rarely stays mad for too long, and she brightens immediately at the sight of her food.

"Thanks, I'm starving," she says, and pulls me into the room. She sits on her bed and breathes in the steam from her fajitas. "Is Dad up there? Does he look mad?"

"You could just come up and see for yourself. He's making root beer floats."

"I can't." Ysabel shakes her head decisively. "There's no point. I don't know what to say yet, and it'd just be . . . weird."

"Well, don't leave it too long," I warn her. "It's better if you get it out of the way before you go to bed . . . you know."

"I know." Ysabel looks uncomfortable. Mom and Dad always say that family shouldn't go to bed angry with each other. Until this thing with Dad, none of us ever did.

"Well." I tap out a rhythm on the doorframe, not sure what else to say. "That float's calling my name. I ate your beans and rice, but if you want something else, I'll make you a—"

Ysabel smiles wanly. "Doesn't matter. I'm not that hungry."

Upstairs, Dad has put my float on a coaster in front of the couch. I stretch out and enjoy it. We watch some old police show with random car chases and explosions. I spoon up my float, not really caring that I missed the first ten minutes of the show and am not sure what's going on. It's not one of those shows where the plot really matters anyway.

When it's over, Dad stands and stretches. "Here, Buddy," he says, and tosses me the remote. He grabs his glass and pads into the kitchen, yawning. I channel surf while I listen to him open the fridge. The hiss of the soda opening makes me smile. Dad really is a glutton for root beer floats.

Instead of coming back to his chair in front of the TV, Dad leaves the kitchen and heads downstairs. Inside, something I didn't even know was tensed up relaxes. I hear the muffled sound of knocking, and a moment later, my father reappears. He looks at me and raises his eyebrows.

"Ready for a refill?"

"I've got it," I tell him, and he nods and flops back in his chair.

I'm rinsing my glass when I see Ysabel standing nervously at the top of the stair, holding her untouched float with both hands. Setting the glass down on the dining room table, she stands rigidly in the middle of the room. Dad mutes the television.

"I'm sorry, and I know I need to offer you meaningful restitution," Ysabel recites quickly, "but I don't really know what that's supposed to mean."

"Ysabel," Dad interrupts. "Do you know I love you?"

My sister looks away. "Dad, I'm not really up to a psychology exercise."

Dad shakes his head. "Well, that's a relief, since that's not what I'm doing."

"Then why are you asking me?" Ysabel's voice is troubled.

"Because I need to be sure that you know that I do," my father replies.

Ysabel clasps her hands together in front of her, twisting her fingers. "I didn't see anything," she says quietly. "I swear I didn't."

Dad winces and looks away. There's a moment of silence. "Thank you for that," he says finally. "It doesn't matter, though. I shouldn't have locked the door."

"It's your house."

Dad looks at Ysabel and smiles. "True. Do you know I love you now?"

Ysabel shrugs warily. "All right, yes. I know you love me."

"Good," Dad says, and unmutes the TV.

Confused, Ysabel stands staring at him a moment, then gives me a bewildered look. I shrug and put away the root beer.

I don't know if that means he's not mad anymore or what. I don't get Dad these days, either.

Revelations

Ysabel

Justin yawns and slides into the backseat next to me. "You ready for this?"

"I guess," I shrug. This morning there's a thin fog obscuring the blue of the sky, and I pull the sleeves of my sweatshirt over my hands. "I'm not sure it matters if I'm not. You?"

"I'm ready," Justin says as Dad backs us out of the driveway, "but Dad's never been rafting."

"We'll be with a group and have a guide, oh ye of little faith." My father grins. "Give me a little credit here."

I'm still shaking my head at the whole concept when we

get to Dr. Hoenig's office. Rafting. What are we thinking? The whole man-versus-wilderness thing is just not a Nicholas family tradition. Dad said Great-aunt Wilma never let him join the Boy Scouts, because apparently she didn't want him to learn to set fires, so Dad never learned to be the hunting/camping kind. The only time Mom likes to be out in nature is in a park with food and a blanket, so we just don't do much in terms of roughing it.

"It'll be fun," Dad insists as he maneuvers into a parking space. "I'm making up for not taking you camping when you were little."

"You did," Justin says.

Dad shakes his head as he turns off the ignition. "Well, I don't remember that."

"He's blocked it from his mind," I announce, stooping to tie my shoe, then jogging to catch up. "Don't you remember that father-son thing at church?"

"That wasn't camping," Dad argues as we walk into the office. "We were in a cabin."

"There was wildlife, though," Justin says, then winces. "Monster mosquitoes."

"And spiders in the shower," Dad says, grinning. "I could barely get you to bathe that weekend."

"Dad, I was *eleven*," Justin reminds him. "It was about the *shower*, not the spider."

"Good morning, Nicholas family." Dr. Hoenig's eyes crinkle with her smile. She motions us into the office, closing the door behind us. "Is it safe to say you're a much happier group this morning than you were yesterday?"

"He's decided to drown us," I tell her, and flop into the armchair closest to the door. "We're going rafting."

"Ah, the TransParent trip up to Whalin Glen." The

gray-haired woman makes a regretful face. "I wish I could go, but there just aren't enough hours in the day. Shall we get started? Can I offer you something to drink?"

"We're fine," Dad assures her, taking his customary seat on the end of the couch.

Maybe *he's* fine. But I'm feeling stupid. How could I have forgotten about the other transgender people Dad wanted us to meet?

Dr. Hoenig says she wants to "check in" with each of us and starts by asking Justin how he's doing. I stay tuned out, my mood dark, as I worry pointlessly over the raft trip. There are a thousand ways to make a fool of yourself in front of strangers, and I just know I'm going to suck at rafting. What if we're the only normal people there?

"You've gotten pretty quiet, Ysabel. How are you feeling about things this morning?"

"Fine." I smile nervously, hoping she didn't notice I was paying zero attention to her just now. "I'm not really awake."

Dr. Hoenig chuckles. "Have you had a chance to start working on your list of rights?"

"Uh, no," I admit, tucking my foot under my other leg. "I forgot all about that."

She nods, then turns to my brother. "What about you, Justin? Any thoughts yet?"

"I'm done. First on my list is 'The right to know what's going on,' " Justin says.

I glare. When did he have time to work on a list? "Did you just come up with that?"

"No, I did not just come up with this," Justin says, offended. "I thought of it yesterday when I woke up."

116

Oh. About the time I was snooping, trying to find *out* what was going on.

Dad shifts on the couch. "'What's going on' seems pretty broad. Could you be more specific?"

"That's a good point," Dr. Hoenig says, and leans back in her seat. "The best thing you can do with these lists of rights is make them detailed and clear. So, Justin, you want to know what's going on. With whom?"

"Okay." Justin sits forward intently. "I have the right to know what's going on in terms of plans that affect my life, my routine, and my, uh, well-being." Justin nods to himself. "I think that covers it."

"Ysabel, do you agree with that?"

I shrug. "I guess."

Dr. Hoenig raises her eyebrows. "So you don't agree with all of it?"

I heave a sigh. "No, I agree with all of it. I'm just . . ." I let the words trail away.

"What's the matter with it?'" Justin protests. "I covered everything."

"I know. It's fine, but . . ." I look at Dr. Hoenig. "This whole thing's kind of pointless."

She gestures. "Keep talking."

"Justin and I don't really have rights, no matter if we sit here and pretend that we do. Dad's just going to do whatever, and he and Mom are going to decide where we live and those kinds of details, and until we're legally of age, we just have to go along with it or find a foster home."

"Well, that's grim," Dad mutters, pushing up the sleeves on his shirt.

"No, it's *true*." I straighten in my seat. "First, you and Mom split up. Then, Mom starts trying to sell the house—*without even asking us*—and Poppy won't even consider letting us move in with him and Grandmama, because you and Mom have already figured out we're all moving—never mind if I can find another welding teacher or if Justin can find a good debate team—"

"Hold on a minute." Dad leans forward. "What do you mean, 'we're all moving'? You're not moving, Ysabel."

"Now, see?" I'm irritated. "How much easier would our lives have been if you'd just said that to begin with? Just a few statements like 'You kids aren't moving. We're not getting a divorce. Everything's going to work out.'"

"How was he supposed to know everything would work out?" Justin interrupted. "It's not like anyone ever knows that."

"It's not like anyone ever knows everything that has to do with their well-being, either, but you don't hear me criticizing *your* list," I retort.

"Time-out," Dr. Hoenig says quickly, a slight smile on her face. "There are too many good points being brought up here to miss. Now, Chris, this seems like an ideal moment to give a few statements that you can make—apparently the consensus here is that there's been too much confusion and not enough information. So, let's have three simple statements from you."

Dad straightens up to oblige her. "One: no one is moving. Two: no one is getting a divorce. Three: no one is selling the house."

"Then what's with all the Realtors?" Justin interrupts. "I've talked to the same lady three times."

Dad opens his mouth, then closes it, frowning. "Three times? We were pricing places a while back," he admits finally, "but that's done. They shouldn't still be calling."

Justin and I exchange looks. "Oh," I say, feeling stupid.

"See? No mystery," Dad says, his voice smug. "You can always ask if there's something you want to know."

"There's some stuff you don't want to have to ask," Justin mutters.

"Like what?" Dr. Hoenig encourages him.

Justin glares at Dad. "Like, 'Is that my dad in drag at my debate event, or have I lost my mind?'"

I wince. Justin has never quite forgotten that I didn't believe him that day.

Dad's expression is troubled. "Buddy, you should never have had to ask that. I'm so sorry. That entire day was a disaster. My flight was delayed, and I was already late. I thought if I took the time to change, I'd miss the whole thing."

"You knew! You watched me walk off that stage, and you didn't even say anything." I hear the accusation in my voice.

Dad shakes his head. "I couldn't say anything. I couldn't face you." He sighs. "If it hadn't been for Poppy catching up with me on my way back from Robinson, I might not have ever said anything." He looks at Justin. "I just wanted to forget it happened. I figured you wanted that, too."

Justin looks away, tacitly refusing to meet his eyes and ease the ache in his voice.

Silence stretches. None of us know what else to say.

"We've had a lot of things get swept under the rug in the last few months, Nicholas family," Dr. Hoenig finally says quietly. "A lot of things we've been afraid to ask, a lot of things we've not wanted to face. Tomorrow, let's see how much progress we can make toward getting down to bare floors."

As if on cue, the three of us stand. Dr. Hoenig opens her door, and we file out.

* * *

It's an hour later when Dad breaks the silence.

"This is it," he says, braking and signaling left. We turn off of the tree-lined road onto a graveled lot. In the distance a tall bridge arches over a wide, muddy expanse of river. A few people are pulling inner tubes down the steep embankment toward the water below, and others stand around cars, changing shoes and slapping on sunscreen.

We drive through the lot kicking up dust. I raise the window hurriedly, and Dad slows as rocks spray out from under the tires. A guy near a battered orange and white striped van waves, and Dad waves back, almost windmilling his arms in the confined space near the windshield.

I give the group a guarded glance as we pass. There are ten or fifteen people standing there, most of them adults, with a couple of little kids by the hand. Dad turns into a parking space and throws open the door, practically before the engine stops.

"Morning!" bellows a tall, tanned woman with a shapeless bush of sun-bleached hair. She's the lady Dad introduced me to at the street fair, and I strain to recall her name. Trina? Tina?

"Sorry we're late," Dad calls. He pops open the trunk and digs around in its depths. The car bounces, and the back window is obscured as Dad hauls out whatever he's got in there. A few people from the group move over and stand around the back of the car, chatting and laughing with Dad. Justin exhales and looks across the car at me, tension on his face.

"This is it, huh? The big meet up."

I look at my brother and try to smile. "Yeah. I guess we should get out?"

Happy Trails

Justin

The air smells like hot asphalt and dust. I get out cautiously, pulling my backpack up on one shoulder and looking at the people leaning on their cars and talking in little groups.

Dad's friend comes around the car and gives me a huge smile. I give her a nod, taking in her Nordic giantess look. She's taller than I am, and the long, bare legs beneath her black shorts are tanned and muscular. Her red golf shirt has letters on the pocket that make it look like a uniform.

"You must be Justin. I'm Treva," the woman says, holding out her hand. I give it a quick shake and drop it, not much in the mood for meeting new people or making small talk.

"Nice to meet you," I say. Her voice is no lower than Mom's, and something in me relaxes a little.

"Good to see you again, Ysabel." Treva smiles, waving as Ys comes around the back of the car to stand next to me. "Boy, you both look just like your daddy."

"We're *nothing* alike," I'm quick to point out. Her innocent observation doesn't set well. Right now I'm not ready to be related to my father.

"I'm sure you're your own man," Treva says calmly, giving me a half smile. "You ready to hit some rapids today?"

"Rapids?" Ysabel exclaims. "Nobody said anything about rapids."

"They're not too intense." Treva laughs, moving toward her. "There are a couple of spots where it gets pretty fast, but we're not talking miles of white water here, just a couple of exciting spots. I've been a guide for years, and I'll tuck you up in my boat and make sure you stay dry."

"No, thank you," Ysabel says quickly. "I'll just go with Justin."

"We'll probably all be stuck on the same raft anyway," I tell her. "There's something like seven people per raft, right?" I turn back to Treva for confirmation.

"Six, usually. We're expecting about thirty-eight people, and some of the kids will just be non-paddling passengers." Treva looks up as a dusty white bus lumbers into the lot. "I think that's our ride to the riverhead. Chris! You ready?"

"I'm ready," Dad says from right behind me. I twitch, feeling the hairs on the back of my neck stiffen. I resist turning around to look at him. His silence since we left Dr. Hoenig's office lets me know that he's feeling bad, but I'm not ready to care yet.

We crunch across the parking lot, puffs of dust following. It's already really dry in this part of the state, and I'm grateful I'm wearing Dad's old running shoes and not mine as I see a wet swimmer climbing up the bank from the river and watch the fine white dust turn into sticky mud beneath his feet.

I buff the toe on the leg of my pants and then frown. Ysabel thinks I'm obsessive about my shoes, but I just like my kicks to be clean. That's not an issue, is it? Is Dad this particular about his clothes? Was that the first sign that he was . . . turning into Christine? How do you know, even when you're little, that just because you like a tiara you're going to be like this?

I shake my head. Now is not the time to be thinking of Dad.

At the bus stairs, Treva stands with a clipboard next to the driver, and the two of them converse. A couple of guys start lugging boxes over, and the driver bounds down the bus steps to unlock the under-bus storage. I expect to see rafts loaded, but there's only big boxes, a cooler, and a couple of folding tables.

Bored, I take in the crowd moving toward the bus. There's a little bit of every population—dark- and fair-skinned folks, both curvy and thin, and all kinds of body art; dreadlocks and dye jobs, mixed in with military-length flattops and shaved heads. I'm surprised to see so many little kids here. Most of them are hanging on their parents' arms and bouncing around, playing with the dirt, but I see at least a couple of guys our age. A tall guy with wavy brown hair stares at me openly, then turns and mutters to the big blond kid next to him.

O-kay. So, are they judging me or scoping me out? Am I going to be hit on by gay guys or what? I hate this day already.

123

"Hey, Chris!"

I turn at the shout to see Dad's expression lighten as a man makes his way from a car that's just pulled in, a girl trailing hesitantly behind him. The man's dark hair is in a silver-streaked military buzz, and he is ripped and tanned in his sleeveless shirt, his dark eyes energetic. His grin is lively and vigorous in contrast to the girl, who is thin and wiry and stands listlessly next to him, saying nothing. She looks normal enough—like a girl, I mean—but I look closely, trying to be discreet. She squints out at us from beneath a massive sun hat that covers most of the top half of her face.

She's hiding. She must be a transperson.

"Hey, Ike," Dad greets them, slapping hands with the other man. "How are you, Bethany? Let me introduce my kids." Dad smiles. "Guys, this is Isaac Han and his daughter, Beth. My kids, Ysabel and Justin."

"Nice to meet you," Ysabel says, ducking slightly to see beneath Bethany's hat. I give her a look at her rudeness, but she only gives me a slight shrug, as if to ask, "What?"

I shake Mr. Han's hand and read the ink just above his collarbone: *To Thine Own Self Be True.* "Shakespeare on a tat. Cool."

"They're some good words to live by," Mr. Han says seriously, and nods. "Nice to meet you, Justin. Heard a lot about you and your sister."

My smile vanishes. *Heard what?* I'm sure I don't want to know.

Dad and Mr. Han chat casually about nothing. They make an odd pair; as big as Dad is, he looks almost skinny next to Mr. Han. I wonder how much I'd have to work out to be that cut, and realize regretfully that outside of dropping out of school and devoting myself to buffing up all day, I probably don't have that kind of time. Mr. Han must be a personal trainer or something.

Ysabel, Beth, and I stand around awkwardly, silent as the dads laugh loudly at some joke Mr. Han's told. Finally Ysabel attempts to peer beneath Bethany's floppy hat again.

"So, Bethany. What year are you?"

"Sophomore." Bethany's voice is quiet and lower than I expect.

"Us too," Ysabel says. "You live around here?"

Bethany shakes her head. "In Pleasant Hill," she says. "Almost an hour from here."

There's a slightly friendlier silence, then Beth asks, "You live with your dad now?"

"No," Ysabel and I say in unison.

"I mean," Ysabel says hurriedly, "we're just visiting. We might be staying with him sometimes, but"—she shrugs uncomfortably—"we don't know what's happening yet."

"Actually, we won't be staying," I put in, giving Ysabel a look. She gives me a quick frown, as if I've said too much of our private business in public, but the truth is, we're *not* staying. *I'm* not staying, anyway.

And Bethany just nods, as if Ysabel hasn't been babbling and we haven't just been having a silent fight.

Before I have too long to wonder about that, Treva calls out family names and checks them off her list on the clipboard. Dad gives a wave when she calls our name, and soon, it's clear we're all accounted for.

"Let's roll!" she shouts, and waves people toward the bus. The last of us in the group make our way toward the vehicle, pale beige under the layer of grime coating the back end. Ysabel puts two or three people between us and Dad before she ducks in front of me and mounts the steps. She chooses a seat near the back and dumps the yellow life jacket on the seat to the floor. After opening the window, Ysabel collapses into the green vinyl seat.

Treva, somehow, is right behind us. She drops into the seat across the aisle from us. "So, you guys," she begins, including Ysabel in her friendly smile. "You rafted before?"

"No. What's your shirt say?" In debate team, Mr. Lester says that going on the offensive is sometimes the best way to make your opponent give something away involuntarily. I watch for the quick blink that shows Treva switching mental gears.

"It's my company," she answers, holding her sweatshirt away from the well-endowed curve of her chest to give me a better view of the embroidered black logo: "*en | GNDR*—it's just another way to say 'engender.'"

My eyebrows jump, hearing the word made from the stylized letters. "Are you one of Scanlon's clients? Does my dad work for you?"

Treva laughs. "Good grief, no. *This* is my business." She gestures. "This group. I run outdoor activities for TransParent and a few other special groups."

"So, transpeople only want to hang out with other transpeople?" Ysabel asks. "Great."

Treva shakes her head. "I doubt that. It's just, sometimes, gay or lesbian people or transpeople want to simply be themselves and have fun, and . . . *other* people can make that difficult."

Ysabel slumps back. "Oh." She straightens, then blurts, "So, do you mind if I ask you a question?"

Treva flicks a glance toward where Dad is sitting, then grins.

"I guess your dad didn't mention it. I am a transsexual person," she says. "Was that what you wanted to know?"

"I knew it," Ysabel mutters.

I check out Treva's chest again, then clench shut my eyes. They *look* real.

"I'm an MTF," Treva continues. "MTF, if you're not familiar with the term, means—"

"Male-to-female," Ysabel interrupts. "So, you used to be Theo or something."

"Travis," says Treva, with a wry look. "You okay with that, or are you panicking?"

Ysabel just shrugs. "Whatever."

Treva glances over. I gulp and manage to keep my eyes above her neck this time. "No," I manage finally. "I'm, uh, not panicking." Not much, anyway.

Treva gives a businesslike nod. "A transitioning parent can be a lot to adjust to, but I'm glad to see you're here, giving it a shot."

I immediately change the subject. "So, what's all the stuff you loaded under the bus?"

Treva's eyebrows waggle. "Lunch," she says, "and super-secret items."

"Paddles, probably." Ysabel rolls her eyes.

"Nope, not paddles," Treva corrects her. "The rafts are already waiting for us."

Just then, the bus driver hollers a question, and Treva stands. "Duty calls, friends. See you on the river."

Still Waters

Ysabel

The switchbacks on the gravel road raise clouds of dust that sift into the old bus windows. The window in front of us drops into its aluminum casings with a clatter as we round a corner, and the pair of women in the seat ahead of us surge to their feet to close it, laughing and coughing and batting the dirt off of each other's clothes.

I examine their thin, wrinkled necks and frosted hair and narrow my eyes. They look like someone's grandmas. They can't be transgender or transsexual people, or whatever Treva calls it.

I'm not surprised that Justin's staring at them suspiciously. When our eyes meet, he gives me a slight shrug and goes back to his examination, as if determined to discover . . . something.

We're surrounded by a sea of zinc-slicked noses and sun visors, and I can't help but stare, trying to figure out whose face might be fooling me, whose happy smile is a cover for a life that might surprise me. My count is shaky; I come up with first one, two, three, then revise my count to two, then four.

No one else on the bus seems concerned about anything. Everyone else is laughing and talking or looking out the windows. A couple of people are holding up cameras and snapping away, modeling their ugly life vests. I tamp down another surge of confusion, shaking my head at my silly thoughts. *Everyone looks so normal!* I keep wanting to exclaim.

Of course they do.

After what seems like miles of driving uphill, the bus suddenly pulls off the road into a narrow lane, and the driver sets the brake and kills the engine. The smallest kids whoop and begin unfastening their seat belts. Treva waves her arms for attention and moves toward the middle of the bus.

"Okay, people, listen up," she calls, and the bus quiets some. "We'll get out of the bus, we'll stay off the road, and we'll get into groups of six. If you've got a child under ten with you, you'll need to make sure that you and that child are in Scooter's or Ted's group." She points. Two big guys at the front of the bus stand and wave briefly before sitting down.

"Each group will have one guide, and a couple of them are already down with their rafts. The first thing you need to do when you get down there is fasten your life vests. Do NOT go into the water or do anything else without that life vest on. The second step is your helmet. No helmet, no raft! Buckle it on, folks. We're going to have a good, safe time today, and everyone will have fun if you listen and follow the rules, capiche?"

There's a general laugh as a few people respond to Treva's rusty Godfather imitation. Then, with her leading the way, the general exodus begins.

Justin bounces his leg as people move down the aisle. Dad waves a hand, then is lost in the press of shoulders, backs, beach towels, and the thick cocoa butter scent of sunblock. The women in front of us stand, chattering comfortably as they step out into the aisle. I wait impatiently as they juggle their life jackets, water bottles, waist packs, and visors. Seeing us watching them, one of the ladies shoots me a conspiratorial smile.

"We've never tried white-water rafting before," she confides giddily.

"Well, life is short," Justin says sweetly. "Better get out there and give it a try."

"Oh!" the woman exclaims, looking around and realizing that she's blocking traffic in the narrow aisle. "Here we go."

"Finally," my brother mutters, leaping out of the bus and looking around.

"Where are we supposed to go?" I ask, slipping on my life jacket. Above us, a few thin clouds are whitening the sky, and it's already gotten quite warm.

"Dad just waved at us," Justin says, and I look around, finding him standing near a bright orange inflatable raft with Bethany and her father. Dad catches my eye and waves again.

"You want to go with him?" I ask as Beth and I watch each other uneasily.

"Not hardly," Justin mutters.

"Fine. Let's find someone else." I start down the rock beach. "Maybe that Bethany chick will come. I have a few questions I'd like to ask her."

Justin swivels his head toward me, panic in his expression. "Ysabel, if it's a question like the one you asked Treva, *forget it*. You can't ask people stuff like that."

"I didn't actually *ask* Treva anything," I defend myself. "She volunteered."

Justin shakes his head. "It doesn't matter. Let's just raft, okay?"

"I'm not completely stupid," I insist. "I just wanted to ask her some questions. I mean, if she's on this trip, she's got to know something about this trans thing." I lower my voice. "I promise not to embarrass you."

Justin just grunts.

We're almost to the rafts when we're intercepted by a compact, black-haired girl in a red en|GNDR T-shirt. She shows a quick flash of white teeth as she smiles.

"I think you're the rest of my crew. I'm Tarie Sabado." She hands us each a black helmet. "Has either one of you done any river rafting before?"

"I can paddle a canoe," I offer.

"Well, that's a start," Tarie laughs.

Tarie, our guide, drags us over to Bethany, and introduces us to two other guys, Connor and Marco, who fill up our six-person crew. Connor, who is tall and broad-shouldered with longish blond hair and a dimpled, good-natured grin, seems okay; at least he smiles. Marco just stares at us when we're introduced and kind of grunts. While Tarie gives us a little safety lecture and tells

131

us about paddling, Marco mutters something to Connor, who punches him and laughs silently, his fair skin turning red with the effort to keep quiet. I wonder if they're a couple or if one or both of them is transgender. How does that work?

"Gentlemen?" Tarie's voice is sweet, but the guys give her straight faces immediately.

"Sorry, Taric," Marco says meekly.

After a narrow-eyed look, Tarie starts talking again, and Marco and Connor start messing around again. I glance back at their smirking faces, weirdly reassured. Guys being guys is so boringly *normal*. Whatever else is unusual about this gathering, Marco and Connor are as normal as it gets.

We get the helmets on, a few of us climb in, and the others push the raft out to where it is floating. Tarie gives us a brief lesson on paddling, then we push off, the five of us seated precariously on the damp rubber ledges that double as seats, the guide on her own perch in the back.

Rafting is deceptively hard work. Digging into the clear water with the plastic orange blade of my paddle, I feel the burn of the muscles in my arms and across my back, and I work up a sweat. Rhythm and pacing and watching for rocks crowd out everything else from my mind. In a way, this reminds me of smithing: instead of banging a hammer against heated metal, I'm dipping a paddle in cadence. It's swing—wait, swing—wait, all the same.

Bethany, sitting in front of me, gives a panicky scream as her paddle is almost wrenched from her hand by the current. My stomach swoops as the raft abruptly picks up speed and veers, surprising a shriek out of me. Everything feels out of control as we dip down into what seems like a hole in the water.

"Paddle! Don't stop!" Tarie shouts, and I can hear the laughter in her voice as all of us make sounds of dismay.

"Dig!" Marco shouts from the front of the raft, and on his count, I dig in on the left. Connor digs in on the right, as does Justin, and Beth frantically alternates strokes. Pretty soon, the wild spinning takes on more of a definite direction, and we pop out of the hole—and head for what looks like a boulder.

"Lean!" everyone screams, and we all lean in different directions. No one is paddling anymore, and the raft begins to spin sideways.

"Right! Lean right!" Tarie hollers. I wrench myself to the right. We barely miss being plastered, scraping by the stone with frantic pushes from our oars. Fortunately, on the other side of the rock, the water slows. Our raft bobs in place for a moment, and we stare at each other with shocked expressions.

"I thought we were so dead," Bethany gasps out.

"We almost were. Where the hell did that rock come from?" Marco's face is slack.

It's weird how speed jolts everything else out of your head. Now Marco and Connor turn from the bow and exchange shaky smiles with the rest of us like we're all friends. Relief makes us a little giddy.

"You okay, Ys?" Justin's grin is wide.

"I'm good," I reassure him, adjusting my helmet. There's a scrape on my arm where I got bushwhacked, but other than my accelerated pulse, I'm all in one piece.

"Okay, folks, that was just the warm-up," Tarie warns us. "You gave me a heart attack with that rock, but you remembered to lean in time. Connor, you did a great job leading out—keep it up. Everybody ready?"

Even if we weren't, it's too late.

There's nothing you can do when you're on white-water rapids but get through the run you're in, and the next one, and the next one. After the first two, my arms are shaking, and I realize I've been screaming. Other rafts flash by, spinning through the current. At one point, I hear Dad's laugh and watch as he and Mr. Han lean into a turn and disappear.

At the end of the next run, Tarie laughs at our shaken expressions. "Rest up!" she shouts, her dark eyes electric with eagerness. "Bucktooth, comin' atcha!"

All the rapids have such dumb names, like Beelzebub's Blender, Spin Cycle, and The Maw. Between them, the water eddies along, slowed to a whisper of its roar, and we rub our arms and relax, talk excitedly about the near misses, the granite-walled scrapes, the branch whippings and stomach-clenching plunges and sheer terrors of the last run. And then, the water picks up speed again.

By the time we come to our fifth run, we find out that not everyone has fared so well. We come out of a narrow chute just after Churner, and we mount a rescue that includes a laughing couple of old dudes and some embarrassed girls, all of whom said that they'd rafted before. "It's just bad luck," they assure us cheerfully.

A mile or so later, we narrowly avoid colliding with another raft, filled with dripping riders. The group is boosting one last person back onto the raft. Among the bedraggled crew are the two ladies from the bus.

"Are you guys all right?" I yell, feeling a little guilty for being still mostly dry.

"We're just fine," the guide calls back. "We'll dry out at dinner."

"When is dinner, anyway?" Justin turns around to ask.

"It's literally just around the bend," Tarie reassures him.

"Land, ho!" Marco bellows. Tarie hollers and waves at the other guides, who are pulled in to a cove with a line of tables and some coolers set up near piles of bleached driftwood and big rocks.

"Thank God," mutters Bethany. Her thin arms are criss-crossed with welts, and her ponytail is plastered to her sweaty back. We all look a little worse for wear.

I dump my helmet and jump out, eager to help the beaching crew, and just about manage to capsize the raft. Tarie has to wade downstream to recover my paddle, and my backpack gets a little wet, but eventually our raft is secured.

I'm grateful for the bins filled with packages of unscented wipes and antibacterial hand wash. A staff member points out the blue portable toilets high up the hill above the beach, and after a super-fast but necessary trip, I wipe down hands and bare, muddy legs and feel a little more human.

Bethany follows me to a driftwood log, hissing as she cleans her scratches.

"Beth!" Her father hurries over, his tanned face creased in concern. He squats next to us and peers at his daughter's arm. "What happened? Those scratches look bad."

"I'm fine," Beth mutters, and I give her father a sympathetic smile.

"It's from a bush," I tell him. "It would have been worse if we'd hit that first rock."

"How are you, Bel?" Dad's knees are suddenly at my shoulder. "Ready for supper?"

"I'm waiting for Bethany," I say, looking him over. His clothes are dry, and he appears only slightly rumpled and sweaty. "You guys didn't tip?"

"Nah, we're professionals," Dad brags, stretching his arms above his head. "I could stay out here all the time, if it was always this nice. Let's eat. We'll save Beth a spot in line."

"I'm coming now," Bethany says quickly, standing. She scans her arms for additional scratches, then shoves her hands in her pockets.

"So, what happened to those arms, Beth?" Dad asks as he falls into step with us.

"We got sucked down a chute sideways," Beth replies with a little shrug. "I got scraped into a tree. As long as it's not poison ivy or something, I'll be fine."

Beth's father, walking on the opposite side of her, frowns. "They don't look fine. I want you to go to the first-aid table. They have antibacterial cream. You don't want those to get infected."

"They're not that deep," Bethany says stubbornly, crossing her arms, then wincing.

"That's it." Mr. Han grasps his daughter's arm with gentle but insistent fingers. "We'll catch up with you guys later. Beth is going to get these looked at."

"Geez, Mom," Bethany bursts out angrily. "Are you even listening? I said they're *fine*."

"We're going to take five minutes to make sure you don't end up with infected welts all over your arm," Mr. Han retorts, and drags his protesting daughter away.

Mom?!

"Belly." Dad's voice is quiet.

I realize I've not only stopped walking, but I'm staring like a five-year-old. Quickly I turn away, hundreds of comments and observations crowding onto the tip of my tongue.

I close my mouth on all of them.

"Ready to eat?" Dad asks, his hand light on my shoulder.

"Mm-hmm," I say, and keep walking.

Happy Hour

Justin

Dad's running shoes—which are sandy and filled with river water—are trashed. Ysabel's hair is standing out from her face like a frizzy lion's mane, and I've got sweat stinging my eyes.

Everything is awesome.

"I'm going to get seconds," I announce.

"Get me some chips," Ysabel requests, and I stagger to my feet, wondering if our raft is going to float after everything we're putting away. Marco is in line ahead of me, and I've seen him here at least twice.

By now, the eaters have dwindled to a few diehards like me

and people coming back for seconds on ice cream sundaes—Treva's super-secret treat that was packed in ice chests under the bus. Some of the little kids are gathered near the beach, wearing towels on their heads and stick fighting. Dad wandered off in that direction, but all I want to do is eat and catch some z's before we get on the water again. Tarie said the last eight miles before the bridge are the wildest. I believe her.

I put together a couple of massive hoagie sandwiches on soft rolls and grab a bag of chips for Ysabel and one for myself. Bethany is wandering over, her face covered by her hat again. Marco follows her, balancing two giant peanut butter cookies on his can of soda.

"Hey, Beth." Ysabel grins. "I don't see any bandages."

"I took them off." Bethany's voice is a low growl. She snatches off her hat and collapses on the log next to Ysabel. "He drives me crazy."

I drop Ysabel's bag of chips in her outstretched hand and sit next to her on the sandy ground. "That's what parents are for. It's in the contract."

"You just need a little brother or something," Marco says, leaning back on his elbows. "It'd spread the love around."

"It's insane." Beth rakes her fingers through her ponytail, then pulls out her hair tie and begins to braid her hair. "He's always on my case with the sun hat, the homeschooling, the tae kwon do—he's convinced something's going to happen to me. Either I'll get skin cancer, or fail calculus, or get kidnapped or something."

"What? You're already taking calculus?" I blurt, dismayed.

"Justin." Ysabel rolls her eyes. "Forget the calculus, all right? The woman is venting."

139

"Sorry." I shake my head. "It's just that I can't take calculus till junior year."

"You actually *want* to take calculus?" Marco stares. "That's sick, man."

Bethany looks flustered. "It's just math," she says hurriedly. "I shouldn't be complaining. Homeschooling works better for us now, anyway. Mom travels a lot."

"Do you go with your mom?" Ysabel asks curiously. "Or do you stay with your . . . other parent?"

"Nope, it's just Mom and me," Bethany says. "Dad bailed on us a long time ago."

I blink, trying to follow the conversation thread. "Wait, you call your mom 'him'?" I ask, then wave my comment away. "Sorry. Forget it." I'm picking up Ysabel's bad habits.

Bethany looks defensive. "Well, why shouldn't I call him Mom? He's always going to be my mother, isn't he? I mean, a mother is the one who carries you all that time, who gives birth to you, the whole deal. Nothing changes that, no matter what body he's in, so . . ." She shrugs.

"Uh, yeah." I nod, trying to imagine Mr. Han's buff body pregnant. "That's true."

"I wish I had your mom's biceps." Ysabel changes the subject. "Do you do weights, too?"

Bethany holds out her skinny arms, indignant. "Does it *look* like I do weights? I avoid sweat and grunting as much as possible. Mom's the one who likes the gym."

"But you still sweat doing tae kwon do, right?" Connor wanders over with a bag of chips and folds himself down to the ground between Beth and Marco.

"Two years this May," Bethany says. "I have a green belt, with a blue stripe."

"Cool. This is my fourth year in jujitsu," Connor offers. "I'm testing for green belt in two weeks."

"Is that like a rule or something? Every kid who's with Trans-Parent has to do some martial art?" Bethany and Connor laugh, and I shrug. "Well, I just wondered."

From down the beach, a little kid with a soccer ball waves his arms and hollers, "Marco! Come play with me! Marco!"

"Later, Ruben," Marco yells, and stretches out on his back.

The little boy comes closer, looking uncertainly at the rest of us from beneath his mop of wavy brown hair. "Marco," he begins mournfully, "you *promised*."

Marco groans, shoving a last bite of cookie in his mouth and struggling to his feet. "All right, *mijo*," he grumbles, then rolls his eyes at me. "When would I have time for martial arts? I spend my whole life babysitting."

"Now, you boys play nicely," Connor advises, then ducks Marco's kick at his head.

I down the last of my chips and crumple the bag, looking across the beach for a garbage can. Marco has managed to collect half the little kids and is organizing them into a soccer tournament. A few adults are gathering to sit in a polite half circle around the stick-fighting kids, who appear to be acting out a play. There's a lot of gesturing and running around.

Connor follows my glance and smiles. "These trips are so fun for little kids. They get to be the center of attention for a whole day. Sometimes the staff does face painting or brings stuff for a craft. It's pretty cool, if you're eight."

Ysabel asks, "So, how long have you been coming to these?"

"Since I was eight," Connor says, and laughs. "Maddie and Mom couldn't make it today, but if they were here, you'd have gotten the whole story—how they met Treva when she was just starting out, how they decided this was a great program for our whole family. They're big supporters. We go backpacking with a group every summer."

"We've only been coming a couple of years," Beth says, tucking a tendril of hair behind her ear. "It's cool."

I open my mouth to ask Connor about his parents, then hesitate, glancing over at Bethany. It's obviously not a secret that Mr. Han was once a woman, so I take a chance. "Beth, can I ask you about your mom?"

Bethany stiffens. "What about him?"

Her expression is hostile, letting me know I've overstepped. I lean back. "Sorry. Forget it."

"No, go on." Bethany raises her eyebrows. "We covered that I still call him Mom. Do you want to hear about his chest-ectomy? Or did you want to ask about the below-the-waist surgeries? Or the hormone shots?" A dull flush climbs her neck.

"Hey." Connor frowns. "You can say no without being a brat about it, Bethany."

"Are we not supposed to ask about each other?" Ysabel's expression is wary. "Is that another TransParent rule we don't know about?"

"No. You can ask." Beth licks her lips and shoots me a quick glance. "I just get tired of people asking. When Mom started the transition, he was . . . open about it. I got a lot of questions at my old school."

"It's not so much about your mom," I reassure her. "I was just going to ask how long it took for things to seem . . . normal." I carefully feel my way through the words. "I know it must be different for everyone; it just seems like—"

"It seems like we're losing Dad, and we're getting somebody we don't even know, and it's all this huge . . . stress," Ysabel finishes, and I nod.

"I know what you mean," Connor says after a little silence, stretching out his legs and leaning back on his hands. "You get used to it. Maddie—my dad—transitioned when I was seven. I was confused for a long time, but I finally understood Dad and Maddie were the same person, and it got better."

Bethany gives an unhappy laugh. "'Better' is a matter of opinion. Most of the time, the stuff with my mom doesn't bother me. He does what he needs to do to be true to himself. But then"—she glances sideways at me—"I think people are looking at me and judging me because of him, and sometimes I can't deal with it."

I shake my head defensively. "I wasn't—"

"I know." Beth looks embarrassed. "I'm sorry. It's been six years, and every time I think I'm over it, I'm not."

"The hardest thing is new people," Connor says, squinting out over the water. "Everybody at school already knows—and we've lived in the same house since I was five. When somebody moves in on our street, though, all it takes is Mom running out to kiss Maddie before she leaves for work, and then they start staring." Connor gives me a half smile, but his dark eyes are bleak. "It's kinda funny sometimes, when people find out. You watch them try to figure out how to treat you. We can tell when they decide we're some kind of deviants by the time Halloween comes around. There are the parents who make their kids cross the street to avoid our house."

"That's really wrong." I swallow. Is this how it's going to be from now on for us?

"More candy for you, Connor," Ysabel says, touching his arm.

Connor snorts, his humor reasserting itself. "Not if Mom has anything to say about it. She hates Halloween. She's a dentist."

"Bummer."

"Entirely."

Marco jogs toward us, trailed by squealing little kids. "Connor," he pants. "Come kick the ball around, dude. You know you want to."

"Not even a little bit," Connor calls back, and grins.

Just then, Marco's coaching term comes to an end. Tarie stands by our raft and waves her arms. "Mount 'em up! Move 'em out!"

Marco immediately scoops up the ball and is dog-piled to the ground by his brother's friends. I dust the sand from my legs and stand, anticipation spreading through me. Tarie said the last runs would be the best.

Bethany, still seated, groans. "I cannot *move*. I am going to be so sore tomorrow."

"What? You're in the *middle*," Connor exclaims. "You hardly have to paddle!"

"Isn't it great?" Bethany says smugly, and vaults to her feet.

It's a lot easier getting into the boat and under way this time. I sit in the bow, and Connor takes my place in the stern, next to Ysabel. Marco seems unbothered by the switch and gives me a quick nod when we finally get in sync. It feels good to get back on the water.

Tarie distracts me, pointing out a raptor riding the thermals far above us. The next moment, I misjudge the depth of my paddle, and it flings water in an arc behind me. Both Beth and Ysabel squeal. "Sorry," I yell before they can snarl at me.

"Next run is Chili Falls," Tarie announces. "Everybody ready?"

The answer is no—there's really no way we could have been ready, since we don't know the run, but we do our best. The next two hours are a blur of churning water and speed. By the time the river widens again to a lazy flow, the bridge where we got on the bus is in sight. I feel a pang of disappointment that the day is almost over.

All of us come in together: a string of orange and gray rafts bobbing along in the cool gray-green water, everyone sunburned, sweaty, wild-haired, and tired. The rafts lie beached in haphazard lines, and everyone pitches in to collect the paddles into stacks.

Beth looks like she's sleepwalking. Marco ends up with Ruben draped over his shoulders. The rest of the little kids have finally run out of steam and lean against the adults, whining a little, but mostly drooping. All of us groan at the sight of the steep trail from the river up to the parking lot.

"Come on," Connor urges, shoving Beth along the trail in front of him. "One foot in front of the other."

"Easy for you to say," Marco mutters.

We climb the short, steep trail up from the river slowly, taking our time behind people moving stiffly, their newly worked muscles already protesting the hours of activity. When we reach the top, we struggle out of our life vests and helmets, stacking them in the large metal containers on the edge of the parking lot. The en | GNDR staff are circulating, making sure everything goes smoothly. I see Treva striding around with her clipboard.

Our group says the polite nice-meeting-you thing. Bethany smiles at Ysabel, and they make tentative plans to get together, since she lives ten minutes from Dad's house. Connor collects phone numbers and makes suggestions that we stay in touch.

Tarie comes by with a brochure that has the en | GNDR event calendar in it. As Connor said, there is a four-day backpack trip planned for a weekend in August. Part of me wishes we could go.

All of me wishes I knew where our family will be in August.

Playing with Fire

Ysabel

The car slowing down wakes me. We've exited the freeway, and I can see a sign that says Buchannan, 38 Miles. We turn left, toward row upon row of hills, shadows coloring them a dull brownish gray in the early-evening light. The high white clouds have gathered in masses, and it looks like it's going to rain.

Across from me, Justin is asleep, his head tilted back against the seat, arms crossed, and legs stretched out. Dad has the radio on NPR, a cultured-sounding mumble interspersed with occasional jazz riffs. I stretch without much movement, wanting to ease the kinks in my neck without letting my father know that I'm awake. I don't want to talk.

Everyone was really nice today. Treva with her eternal clipboard, Tarie with her whacked-out sense of humor, Marco and his cute little brother, Bethany and Mr. Han, and Connor—especially Connor—were great. It seems like it would be so easy to just walk into a ready-made group of Dad's friends and be happy in Buchannan.

I feel hopeful.

Other people survive a divorce. Other girls manage that two-weekends-a-month thing with their fathers. Other kids our age have two rooms, two houses, sometimes even two churches. For the first time, this whole Dad/Christine thing looks doable.

I feel great, until I realize the one thing missing from today. Mom.

Suddenly, I have to rethink everything.

Dad signals and changes lanes. I squeeze my eyes tighter, feeling a headache threatening as I remember what Mom told me at the airport, before we even left.

"Try and have a good week." She'd fallen into step with me, rubbing her bare arms in the cool morning air, smiling faintly. "Try not to . . . ," she started, and I'd stiffened, felt my shoulders get tight.

"Not to what?"

She'd stopped and taken a deep breath. I changed my grip on the backpack and waited, shifting uncomfortably as Dad and Justin headed through the automatic doors to the check-in line. The Sunday morning airport crowd pushed around us, voices sounded over the loudspeakers, and she watched me calmly, a familiar face in a sea of strangers. Mom had run a tired hand through her hair before speaking.

"Just try to remember your father is not the enemy," she'd finally said, her voice even. "We're on the same side. We're fighting what destroys our family. Don't forget that."

I hadn't known what to say. I'd shifted my torch case onto an empty luggage cart and pushed ahead, confused and unhappy. What else is destroying us? Who else decided our family wasn't good enough the way it was? If Dad's not the enemy, who is?

"Ys. Pizza." Justin walks by and kicks the door, the sound a muffled thump. Upstairs I hear the distorted cadence of a news anchor and know my father's sitting with his feet up on the coffee table, blearily watching TV. He decided on ordering pizza because all of us are wiped, and nobody felt creative enough to come up with something to eat.

I narrow my focus on the blob of glass on my mandrel and move it into the flame and out again. The long orange tongue of flame is hypnotic, and I move my hands quickly, using the heat stored in the stainless steel mandrel to compensate for the cooler flame. The basic bead has formed of orange and white glass, and I concentrate, deciding to extend the bull's-eye effect. I reach for a rod of magenta glass and heat it, continuing to turn the bead on the mandrel so that gravity won't pull the bead out of shape.

"Ys." The smell of onions and basil flows into the room ahead of Justin. I flick a glance at him as he sets down the pizza and closes the door. He sits a more than safe distance away from me. "You not hungry?"

"I'll eat in a minute." I lay a thick layer of magenta glass over the white and orange, heating it until the bead is wide and flat. I pick up my steel scissors and check the location of my graphite tool. Perfect.

"—I've been thinking about it ever since we got home. I guess—"

I pull the bead from the heat and make a tiny snip with the scissors. The glass cuts cleanly, and I lay the scissors against the graphite, hoping to diffuse the heat. Into the flame goes the bead, out again. Snip. Heat. Snip.

"—I don't know. Maybe I'm just tired." Justin's voice is lifeless.

"Hmm." I've made seven cuts, rotating the end of the mandrel slightly against the graphite pad, keeping the petals of my little flower flat. The scissors only stuck once; the graphite pad has done the trick. I pick up a rod of white glass and heat it, laying down a short stripe at the end of each petal for a framing effect. It's perfect.

"Screw it." Justin pushes to his feet. "I hate it when you pretend you're listening."

"Sorry. Don't go, Just." I turn off the flame and bend to place the bead in the annealing kiln. I hate having everything in weird places, and I miss my setup at home. I finally found my torchwork mojo, but Justin's gotten me out of my zone. I push my glasses atop my head. "I'm listening. What kind of pizza did we get?"

My brother hesitates, then slides back to the floor with a heavy sigh. "Half was supposed to be veggie, but they goofed. I picked off the chicken."

I make a face and move the small TV table out of the way. "Thanks."

Justin pushes the box toward me. I settle on the floor and grab a slice.

"So, what's wrong?" Justin asks.

I frown, answering through a mouthful. "With me? Nothing." I swallow. "Why?"

"The only time you work with your music on loud and don't pay attention to anyone is when you're upset."

"I'm not listening to music." I take another bite, feeling unaccountably angry.

"When I came in, you were humming loud enough to go deaf."

I scowl, tossing down my pizza. "Who are you, Dr. Freud? I hum. So what?"

Justin raises his eyebrows and shrugs. "Ease up. It just seemed like you were trying to drown me out, and I wondered if you were okay."

"No, I'm not." I pick up my pizza and take a vicious bite. "This day sucks."

Justin thumps his head against the door. "Weird how that happened, isn't it? It was great until we got back."

I swallow, my stomach suddenly rebelling against the lump of cheese, peppers, and onions in my throat. "It was fine until I started thinking about Mom."

Justin sighs. "Today was great. We met some really nice people. But—"

"Yeah. 'But.'" I move the pizza box. "I like Treva. I like Mr. Han. We'd probably really like Connor's Maddie. But—"

"—but, *Dad*." Justin's wordless gesture says it all.

I nod. "I know. And I know that's probably prejudiced or something. To be okay with it when it's somebody else, but not *our* family."

"It *is* prejudiced. And lame. And I don't know how not to feel that way." Justin leans forward, his elbows on his knees. "I don't know how to be okay with it being *our* family. I don't know how to stop feeling scared about the first time I see him up close as Christine. I look at Connor and Beth, and they seem okay. I just want to get to that point, you know?"

The silence stretches. Both of us jerk when Justin's phone beeps.

"Who—" Justin cuts off the question as he pulls out his phone. He flips it open and stares at the message. Then he sighs and drops his arm, his face expressionless.

I lean forward to look at the call screen.

"Callista again?"

"Yeah. She left me a message earlier. Still wants me to call."

Callista and Justin never actually broke up. The indecisive, wistful expression on Justin's face makes me sad for him. "Well, are you going to? Call her?"

"I'm going to take a shower." Abruptly, he's on his feet and at the door.

I kick the pizza box across the room and lean my head against the bed, staring at the ceiling. It's not fair that Justin and Callista are messed up. Justin really, *really* liked her. But how do people date when their lives are like this? How would we explain Dad?

"This day sucks, God," I announce, but God doesn't answer.

"Ysabel!" Dad's voice is strident and grating on my nerves. "I've called you three times! You have thirty minutes to be in the car before we leave for Dr. Hoenig's."

"I'm up," I mutter, rubbing my face. I slide to the end of the bed and check the annealing kiln. Six new medallion beads sit cool and perfect in its depths. I had the idea for a pendant and had made a few trial beads to see which one I liked. I worked until almost two this morning, but I'm happy with how they turned out.

"It's not like it's my spring break or anything," I mutter, throwing open my bag and pulling out a fresh shirt and a pair of leggings. "It's not like I should be able to *sleep in* or anything."

By the time I'm showered and dressed, my hair in a damp and uninspired ponytail, Dad's pounded on my door twice more, and I am in a pissy mood. It's too late for breakfast, I know, so I grab the last half slice of cold pizza and get it down while I'm lacing my boots. My brother is already in the car by the time I come into the kitchen.

"I said thirty minutes," my father mutters, and hurriedly thrusts two wax-papered bundles into my hands. Herding me into the garage, he presses the button to open the door, then hustles around to the driver's seat. "We're going to be late."

Standing next to the car, I take a quick peek inside the wax paper. I see what I expect: two pieces of toast, slathered with mayonnaise, cradling two eggs, over medium, dotted with flecks of black pepper. I close it quickly, my stomach hurling itself toward my throat. "Here," I say, passing it to Justin, who takes both and shoves them into his jacket pocket. My father twists around and glares at me, then closes his eyes.

"Eggs," he says, and his face gets that expressionless expression that means he's angry. Hopefully he's angry with himself—I won't take responsibility for him forgetting that even the smell of soft-fried eggs makes me want to vomit sometimes. That's the breakfast he used to make for *Justin* when he was going to miss the bus, not for me.

"I had leftover pizza," I tell him, sliding into the backseat. Justin is slumped next to me, wearing his sunglasses. Dad starts to say something, then shakes his head and starts the engine. He backs out of his meticulously clean garage and into the May sunshine.

I take a deep breath, fighting the queasiness in my stomach. Justin isn't even eating the eggs, but the air in the car is too warm, and everything is pressing against me. I punch the button and lower the back window. Lifting my chin, I let the wind blast my face, sucking in cold air. I shouldn't have stayed up so late.

"That's not an acceptable breakfast," Dad says abruptly, and I blink.

"What?" My voice is too loud over the roar of the wind. Justin flicks a glance my direction as I roll up the window.

"That's not an acceptable breakfast," Dad repeats. "Just a piece of cold pizza."

I shrug. "It worked for dinner."

"We don't have time to stop," Dad says, looking at me in the rearview mirror. "If we weren't already running late, I'd make sure you ate something. Your mom's been worried about you not being home for meals. I want you to—"

"Dad, I just said I'm not hungry," I interrupt, wondering where all this is coming from. Mom's been talking to him about me? "I'll be fine until lunch."

My father says nothing, turning into the parking garage in front of Dr. Hoenig's office building and practically jerking the key from the ignition. "Let's go," he says brusquely.

I slide out of the car and slam the door in tandem with my brother. The car rocks under the assault of our combined slams, and I know I'm not the only one struggling to keep my temper.

This isn't good. I stand next to the car for a moment, taking a deep breath.

"Ysabel!" My father's voice hits me like a slap. "We. Are. Late."

I blow out a breath and stomp toward the door my father is holding open. God forbid I should have a moment to myself. God forbid we should make Dr. Hoenig miss us for even fifteen seconds.

This is my favorite way *ever* to spend spring break.

Irresistible Force,
Immovable Object

Justin

There are currently 1 Guests and 2 Users online
at Kids of Trans Forum Chat.
Online Users:
Viking
litgirl
JustC

JustC: So, is anybody here dating?
Viking: You asking me out? lol

JustC: Don't swing that way. Srsly, how do u people date?
JustC: With the parent trans. How 2 explain?
Viking: IMHO, u don't have 2 explain crap.
litgirl: . . . Viking, u don't date, do u

"Silence is okay, too," Dr. Hoenig says calmly, leaning back in her armchair. "You all must have had a busy Tuesday."

If it would make a difference, I'd say I wasn't tired, but I've figured out Dr. Hoenig. Anything I say can and will be used to worm inside my head. I keep my mouth closed, and my thoughts to myself.

Instead of texting Callista back last night, I finally called Mom—she acted like I'd given her a heart attack—read stupid jokes from Viking, and tried doing one of Mr. Lester's freewriting exercises to help me think about the future. Maybe it was stupid to quit debate. Mr. Lester still wants me back next year. It might not be so bad to come up north and spend time with Dad—I could use Bethany's help with calculus. Maybe she's some kind of forensics expert, too, and she can give me some pointers to take back home.

And as long as I'm trying to reset my life, I should probably talk to Callista. I think it's pretty safe to tell her that we've had some family stuff going on; it's obvious Dad's up here and Mom's down south. If she's even interested in there being some kind of . . . us, she'll understand if I say I don't want to talk about it.

Won't she?

It felt good last night to focus on something other than right now. Maybe the only way to start being okay with my life is to just . . . live it.

"We went rafting yesterday." Ysabel's voice comes abruptly from the depths of her usual chair by the door. "It was great."

"Whalin Glen really is restful," the therapist says, tilting her head slightly. Her eyes are sharp, despite her mild tone. "At our first meeting, we talked about the number of things that get swept under the rug in this family. Is something new under there today?"

"Excuse us, Dr. Hoenig. I think we're just running on too little sleep and not enough breakfast," Dad says with a jokey little laugh, and I grimace. I hate it when adults say "us" and "we" but don't really include themselves.

"Dad, I said *I had a piece of pizza.*" Ysabel's voice is edged with anger, like a rattler's warning. "It's not *my fault* you can't tell Justin and me apart."

"Oh, I can tell you apart, all right," my father says. "You're the one who stays in bed until the last minute."

Thanks, Dad. I roll my eyes. Ysabel glares at us both. "No, I'm the one who hates your nasty egg sandwiches!"

Dad throws up his hands in exasperation. "Have you *never* made a mistake?"

"You didn't apologize, so how am I supposed to know it was a mistake?" Ysabel goads. "For all I know, maybe you decided we were all going to *suddenly change* what we do. Maybe I have to *like* egg sandwiches now."

I stifle a laugh. Point goes to Ysabel.

Dad's mouth opens, and closes. He pinches the bridge of his nose, and holds it, and I know he is warding off a headache. "Ysabel, I am sorry about your breakfast. I certainly won't make that mistake again."

"Thank you." Ysabel blows out a breath and crosses her arms. "I'm sorry I stayed up late and overslept *during spring break* so we were two minutes late. Can we be done with this now?"

Dr. Hoenig's brows climb to her hairline. "I'm not sure. It seems like a lot of unresolved anger just over breakfast and being a few minutes late."

My father continues to pinch his nose silently. Ysabel gives a slight shrug.

"Well, it could be we're running on too little sleep," she admits.

I snort a laugh, then fake cough, keeping my hand over my mouth. Dad gives me a look that lets me know he's unconvinced.

Dr. Hoenig swivels in her chair. "How are you this morning, Justin?"

"Fine," I say quickly, ignoring the way her smile widens. I don't want her attention on me, and she knows it. "I'm good."

"Okay." The therapist opens her notebook and flips back a few pages. "Before, we went over part of Justin's Bill of Rights. Ysabel, no progress on your list yet?"

"I don't think I'm doing one," Ysabel says.

"Ysabel." Dad sighs.

"It wasn't a requirement," Dr. Hoenig interjects smoothly. "It was intended to be a communication tool. So." She looks down at her notebook again. "Let's see—"

"Dad was telling us Mom wasn't selling the house." I throw the words into the pause, unwilling to leave the choice of topic to Dr. Hoenig. "You said you didn't know why Realtors were still calling."

Dad nods. "About a month ago, your mom and I wanted to

price houses in our area because she was thinking it might be less expensive to move than to build an addition. In this economy, I don't think moving is the answer."

"Wait, why do we need an addition on the house?" Ysabel looks bewildered. "Are we taking renters?"

"What? No." Dad laughs, but gives her an odd look. "No renters. We're putting in another closet, or maybe a big dressing room off the master bedroom. I don't think we can rent that out."

My mouth dries. "The new closet's for Christine."

"What?" Ysabel's eyebrows pinch.

Dad's expression is confused. "Yes. I thought that was understood. I told you that no one was moving or getting a divorce, and your mother and I explained that we're working on being a family. . . ." A curtain of wariness falls over his expression. "You thought I would stay away from you."

There is an abrupt silence.

"Justin," Dr. Hoenig begins, but I ignore her. *Mom's enlarging the closet. For Dad.*

I hear the creak of Ysabel's leather boots as she leans forward and the quiet sound of the couch springs. "Wait—" Her voice cracks. "You're moving home? To stay?"

"In the long run. That's the goal," Dad says, turning to face her. "No one has set a date. We're not going to rush into this. But we thought our family should be together. I want to work on that . . . to be home with all of you."

Another drawn-out silence. Ysabel is perched on the edge of her chair, watching Dad. She looks serious, almost scared. "Well, cool," she says, and her voice squeaks.

Dad rubs his jaw. "Cool, huh?" he repeats with a half smile. Ysabel rolls her eyes.

Dad turns to look at me, and I flinch. Dr. Hoenig tilts her head, trying to see more of my face. I can't stop looking at the patterns in the beige carpet, feeling put on the spot.

"Buddy. Justin." Dad's voice pulls my attention. "Is there—?" He stops, clears his throat. "I'd like to know what you're thinking." He smiles, but tension dissolves it.

I don't know what to say. "Dad, I'm—"

Dad interrupts, his forehead wrinkled with worry or determination. "Doesn't matter if it's not what you think I want to hear. We can't work anything out if we don't talk anything out, right? So—let's hear it. We've got time." He tries the same tentative smile, and though it lasts longer, there is a raggedness to it, as if I've already said something to claw it away. As if I've already wounded him.

Words are colliding in my head, like they do before a debate event. I try to breathe and find my Zen, like Mr. Lester taught me, but it's taking too long, and I can't wait.

So, I steal.

"Okay. What I'm thinking is, why shouldn't you move home? You're always going to be my dad, right? I mean, even in high heels—you're half my DNA . . . you're part of the reason I'm here. Nothing changes that. So." I blow out a breath. Ysabel glances at me, probably hearing the echo of Bethany's words in mine, but I know Beth would forgive me.

I don't know what else to say. I can't hurt Dad, when he wants to come home. I can't hate him for confusing all of my plans. But he *has*. I was going to be okay. I was going to talk to Callista. I was going to just live my life.

I don't know how I can do any of that with Dad back at home.

161

As all this tumbles through my brain, Dad just *breathes*. It's as if his whole body changes as he sucks in a shuddering breath. He practically melts into the couch as his shoulders lower.

"You know I love you both." Dad's voice is hoarse. He looks from me to Ysabel, his words forceful and emphatic. "I don't think you can ever know how much."

Ysabel ducks her head. I swallow uncomfortably as Dad continues, "If we hold on to that, we can weather this. I truly believe that. All we need to do is remember to love, and we'll make it."

"If you start singing that Beatles song, I'm leaving," Ysabel mutters, and blots her eyes with her sleeve. Dad gives a shaky laugh. Ysabel ignores Dr. Hoenig's subtle offer of tissues. Dad takes one, even though he only crumples it in his fist.

Dad blows out a breath. "Listen, guys, I know we're not finished here—I know we have a long way to go before I'm home, before things feel right. But this means everything—that you're willing. It's such a gift. Thank you. Thank you so much."

"Don't even say that. Don't say 'thank you,'" I blurt, honesty pulling the words from me. His gratefulness is like acid on my skin, and I feel a rush of confused rage. "I don't want you to be grateful. I don't even know how long I mean it."

Dad smiles, his face weirdly peaceful. "I know," he says, crossing the room to sink down onto the couch next to me. "I know," he says, putting his arm around me and holding out his other one to Ysabel.

She immediately wedges in on the couch next to him and buries her face in his neck.

"I love you. We'll get through this all right," Dad says, and I try to breathe.

He's wrong. It's not all right. But that's how we sit, with Dr. Hoenig's box of tissues, until our time is up.

In the parking lot, I'm relieved when Dad asks, "Anyone up for a double feature?"

"Me." I wave a tired arm.

"Definitely." Ysabel perks up. "I need popcorn."

Armed with red licorice and chocolate mints from the drugstore, we settle in at the four-screen theater to watch the horror matinee from the fifties. It's all ants—giant man-eaters in black and white, and miles of Technicolor Amazonian ants that strip a rain forest.

We're almost the only people in the theater. Dad props his feet on the seats in front of us and dozes through most of the second feature. I try to watch the movie and turn off my brain.

But my brain stays on, like it always does. When we get home, it's midafternoon, and Ysabel sets up her torchwork on the back deck. Dad finds a ball game on TV, but it feels like too much effort to follow. I go downstairs and flop on my bed.

When my phone vibrates, I groan. I was supposed to call Mom and I didn't. I'm not in the mood to talk to her now. The phone continues to buzz. Sighing, I pick up, knowing Mom will just keep calling or call Dad if I don't answer.

"Yeah?"

"Uh, Justin?"

"Oh, crap. Callista." At the familiar voice, all the air leaves my lungs.

A nervous laugh. "Uh, yeah. Hi."

"Sorry." I clear my throat. "I thought you were my mom."

"Oh." A pause. Callista clears her throat. "I hoped you'd get in touch last night."

"Yeah." I lick my lips. "Sorry, we were out late. I meant to get back to you." I take a deep breath. "What's up?"

Another pause. "Well, I don't know, Justin." Callista's voice is thin. "I was kind of hoping you could tell me."

My neck stiffens with painful tension. "Oh."

Callista continues, her voice quiet. "I mean, not that you owe me an explanation or anything. I just wanted to talk . . . I mean, if you have a minute or whatever."

I close my eyes, and the silence between us goes a heartbeat too long.

"Justin, is it something I did?" Callista sounds resigned. "I mean, if it's a bad time—"

"No." The word explodes from me, fueled by self-hatred and frustration. "You didn't do anything," I say. "It's . . . complicated—" The minute I say the word, I feel sick to my stomach. "That's a total cliché, I know."

"*Life* is complicated, Justin."

"I know. It's . . . Callista, it's not you, okay? I really like you. There's just some . . . stuff going on. My—" I break off, swallowing the word. I can't tell her it's my family—what if she says something to someone at church? I can't tell her it's my father. I can't tell her anything. "I just have to deal with some stuff."

"Okay," Callista says, and I hear something in her voice that makes panic tighten my chest. She wants more. She's waiting for me to explain what "stuff" is supposed to mean.

"It's just some stuff," I repeat stupidly. "It's not something I can go into, okay?"

"Um, okay." Callista's voice is tiny, barely there.

"I'm sorry," I say. "Look, I'll call you when I get home—"

"You don't have to. I've got to go."

"Wait. Callista, I'm sorry—"

When the lights turn off, I know there's no reason to hold the phone anymore, but it's hard to make my fingers let go.

My stomach burns, like fire is clawing up my throat. I want to break something, smash it into dust. Nothing is ever, ever going to be right again.

There are currently 0 Guests and 4 Users online at Kids of Trans Forum Chat.
Online Users:
C4Buzz
Styx
Viking
JustC

JustC: *hates whole world*
Styx: no h8rs.
C4Buzz: woe. What's up?
JustC: Not dating. Can't let people find out about my dad. Just blew off a girl.
Viking: Did she ask about him?
JustC: No—he's coming home. She'll find out. Too smart.
Styx: if she loves u, yr dad dsn't matter.
JustC: a lie. LOVE DOES NT FIX EVRYTHNG
C4Buzz: Lightn up.
Styx: all u need is love.
Viking: JustC, sent u my number again. Call me.

JustC: Can't do this.
Viking: Call me.
Viking: JustC
Viking: CALL ME.
Viking: You still there?

Through the Fire

Ysabel

By a quarter to six, the sun shifts behind the hill, and it's a little too breezy for me to stay on the back deck. It's kind of tricky working with glass outdoors; while I'm pretty sure I'm gathering dust and other impurities into my beads, it might make them look interesting. I'll check what I've got in the kilns tomorrow and see.

Dad's dozing on the couch again, but I wake him up as I haul the chair back to the table and carry my stuff inside. He smiles at me blearily.

"Guess we should start making dinner, huh?" he asks, and yawns.

"Nah." I shake my head. "I don't know about Justin, but I'm not hungry. Too much popcorn. I'll make a pb&j later if I get hungry."

"Sounds like a plan," Dad says, and his eyes slide shut again.

Poor Dad's been dead to the world for most of the afternoon. Today was hard on all of us; I'm happy to just veg out and work, mess with glass, design jewelry, and think of nothing emotional or important at all.

I drag my case back downstairs and think about setting up my station again, but I'm not in the mood. Instead, I get out my latest *Beadworks* catalog and pore over supplies and glass I can't yet afford.

I'm surprised when my phone rings. The ring tone is the generic song that plays when someone I don't know calls. I flip the phone open, frowning.

"Hello?"

"Ysabel? It's Connor."

"Connor! *Hi!*" I feel a rush of giddy disbelief. At home, guys *never* call me.

"Wow." Connor's voice is startled. "You sound happy."

My face gets hot. "Um, I am," I admit with a nervous laugh. "I'm glad you called."

"Wow," Connor repeats. "I— That's—" He hesitates. "I need to find Justin."

I blink, embarrassment igniting into irritation. "Connor, I know we're twins and all, but we're not identical, okay? Justin has a phone, and I know he gave you the number."

"I know. I'm sorry." Connor's voice is serious. "I wouldn't call you to ask about him for any other reason, but I think it's an emergency, maybe. I think I really pissed him off."

I get up and cross the hall, rolling my eyes. "I'm sure he's fine. Justin hardly ever gets mad. He's probably just asleep. Justin. Phone!" I knock sharply and open his door. "Hang on, he's not in here."

"That's what I was afraid of," Connor says.

"What?" I look in the bathroom, which is empty, then go back upstairs. "What do you mean?"

"Justin got upset earlier on the Kids of Trans forum, and I asked him to call me, and he didn't. He won't answer his phone."

Upstairs, Dad's sacked out on the couch, the TV playing quietly in the background. There's no one on the deck, no one in Dad's room, and no one in the garage. I open the side door and walk outside, leaning against the warm plaster wall of the house. "He's not here." I shrug. "He probably went for a run. That's what he usually does when he's upset."

"If he doesn't turn up in an hour or so," Connor says quietly, "I think you should tell your dad."

I feel chilled. "Are you serious? Connor, what happened?"

"I'm not sure. He said something about a girl."

"Callista," I supply. "She's . . . they're close. Or, they were," I correct myself. "I think they're talking again." I shake away my nervousness, remembering the pain in Justin's face when Callista texted him last night. "Look, Connor, Justin would never go anywhere without saying something at least to me. Ever. I'm sure he left a note somewhere."

Connor's voice is unhappy. "If you find him, would you give me a call? It's cool if he doesn't want to talk to me, but . . ."

"Sure. No problem," I say, going back into the house. "I'll look for a note right now."

But there's nothing in the kitchen, no note on Justin's

bed or on the nightstand next to his bed. I don't find his MP3 player, which makes me think he's running, until I find his running shoes.

I text his phone. *Where R U?*

When I hear the ring tone I programmed coming from the bed, I can't breathe.

I'm going to kill him.

"Dad?" My feet thud up the stairs. "Do you know where Justin is?"

Dad sits up, blinking. "What, honey?"

"Justin. Where. Is. Justin." My voice is edged.

Dad rubs his face, more than half asleep. "Don't know. I thought he was downstairs."

"Did you hear the door open?" I ask. "Do you maybe remember him saying he was going for a walk or something?"

Dad shakes his head. "We were both right here, Belly. We would have noticed him coming by."

"I wouldn't have," I remind him. "I was working. I would have heard the door, but I didn't hear anything."

Dad scrubs a hand across his hair. "Well, give his cell a ring, and—"

"It's in his room, and so are his running shoes. Dad, I think he left. Connor called me and said Justin was upset about a girl, and I looked and looked for him, and he's not here, and he didn't tell me anything or leave a note, and I don't know where he would have gone. You've gotta help me look for him."

Dad looks stunned. "Bel, slow down and run that by me again."

I repeat myself, explaining that Connor phoned and said that this was "an emergency, maybe." Dad frowns.

"Bring me Justin's phone," he says abruptly, bending to slip his feet into his shoes.

Dad's pulled on a different shirt by the time I race up the stairs and hand him Justin's phone. Dad frowns as he scrolls through the last calls. "Who's Calli D?" he asks.

"Callista Douglas," I say. "She texted him last night. He was supposed to call her."

He hands me the phone. "Well, she called him a few hours ago. Take a look at the texts, will you? We might be worrying for nothing."

"He hasn't sent any texts since yesterday," I report, scrolling through the messages. "Just somebody named Viking, and I don't know who that is."

"Maybe Connor knows."

"I don't know why he would just go off somewhere," I fret. "Should we call Mom?"

My father swallows hard, and the muscles in his throat are visible. "Not yet. Not yet. This could be nothing, Belly. You know how your brother is when he's thinking." Dad tries to give me a "don't worry" pat on the shoulder, but his hand lands too heavily. His eyes are wide, the whites around them showing clearly as his gaze darts around the room.

"Okay, then. Listen—I'm going to look for him. I'll drive around for a while. If I can't find him walking through town by seven, we'll ask your mom if she's heard from him today. No reason to get her upset."

"Okay." I head for the stairs. "Let me get a sweater."

"No—Belly, you need to stay here so you can call me if he shows up."

"Right." I stop moving and cross my arms. "I knew that."

171

Dad gives me a quick hug and heads toward the garage. "If you think of anything, give me a call," he says.

"I will." A moment later, I hear the garage door lift, then close behind him. I stand in the middle of the room for a moment, holding myself, then I sit on the couch.

Justin's probably just walking around in the neighborhood, I reason to myself. *He'll turn up in a little while.*

But when my phone rings a half hour later, it's Connor.

"Did you find him?" he blurts.

"No," I say, my voice shaking. "Connor, you have to tell me exactly what happened."

Connor hesitates. "Conversations in the chat room are confidential."

"Connor—"

"He's been posting on the forum, and he basically said he'd had to blow off this girl, and that he couldn't do this anymore, and he was afraid she'd find out about your dad when he came home."

"Couldn't do what anymore?"

"I don't *know.*" Connor's voice is tense.

"Dad's driving around looking. If we don't find him by seven, we're calling Mom."

I take a breath. "Connor, where is he? We don't know where anything is in Buchannan, except the theater. Maybe he's at Dr. Hoenig's office?"

"Is that your therapist?"

"Yeah. I should call Dad and tell him to drive to her office."

"Call me when you find him."

"I will."

Dr. Hoenig's office is closed, and when Dad checks, there's

no one in the parking lot. At seven-thirty, Dad finally comes home, a lot more worried than when he started out, and begins making calls.

The hospital has no record of Justin, or of any accidents in the last few hours with John Doe victims. Because Justin is a minor, Dad could file an official report of a missing person, but he's not convinced that Justin is, as the officer said, "a danger to himself or others," and decides to hold off.

Dad describes what Justin was wearing—shorts, a goofy *Hobbits Are Tolkien Minorities* T-shirt, and ratty canvas sneakers. Maybe a windbreaker. We check his room and find his jacket there. The dispatcher assures Dad that the police driving through town will be on a general lookout for a boy of his description.

Finally, Dad explains the situation to Mom, who is surprisingly calm—at first.

"It looks like he just walked off without much of a plan," Dad finishes, regret in his voice. "It's not like him to leave his phone."

Mom's voice on the speakerphone is tinny. "There's a flight at nine. If he doesn't turn up—"

"I'll let you know," Dad says grimly. He rubs his face. "I wish I hadn't dropped off."

"He's not a toddler who wandered away," Mom points out. "He's sixteen, and he should have left a note, taken his phone, and taken responsibility." Now her voice is angry, and I know for sure that she's scared.

Dad glances at me as I start heading downstairs. I can't deal with any more.

"God, where is he?" I whisper, standing in the middle of his room. Justin's things are put away neatly like they are when he's at home, and I go over his room again, sliding my hand under his pillow, looking on the floor beneath the night table, looking in the bathroom—anywhere for a note, a clue, anything. But there's nothing.

At seven-thirty, my phone chirps. Connor.

"Tell me you've heard from him," I beg.

"No." Connor sighs. "I was just calling to see if he was home."

"Dad's at the airport waiting for Mom's flight to come in," I say. "Connor, I don't understand this. Justin's never left me before, ever. When we were little, both of us ran away from home—together."

I can hear the smile in Connor's voice. "How far did you get?"

"To next door," I say, and laugh a little. "She had these little deer statues in her yard we thought were cool. We were gone all of four minutes." I laugh again, but my breath hitches. I press my hand against my chest.

"This sucks." Connor sighs again. "If I could do anything—"

"Can you come over?" I blurt, hating how shaky my voice sounds.

"I'll borrow Maddie's car and be there in twenty minutes."

Checking Out

Justin

"It's just some stuff. It's not something I can go into, okay?"

"Um, okay."

"I'm sorry. Look, I'll call you when I get home—"

"You don't have to. I've got to go."

"Wait. Callista, I'm sorry—"

If I stay in the house another second, I know I'm going to break something. I slip in the earbuds of my MP3 player and flick through my playlist until I find something loud.

There's a low cement wall around a few plants near the curb across the street where I put up my heel and stretch my tight calves, watching a flock of noisy blackbirds threaten a few starlings over the oak tree at the end of the court. I bend forward, putting my head as close to my knee as I can, then switch legs. My muscles are reluctant, burning with strain, and I fill my head with the pain, glad to do anything but think.

I follow the sidewalk beside a row of straight, broad tree trunks. The slightly fuzzy effect of their newly opened leaves makes me think of a little kid's drawing. Everything is so bright and shiny in this neighborhood that it's hard not to smile at the postman walking along ahead of me, stuffing mail and newspapers in the sidewalk boxes. Heading off across the hill behind Dad's town house, I pick up the dusty walking trail and follow it down at a ground-eating lope. The puffs of dust kicking up make me glad I didn't wear my good running shoes.

A few blocks from home, I realize I probably should have called Viking—who I discovered was Connor when he sent me his number. He's a good friend so far, but I don't think I can explain how I feel about this. The people in the chat room mean well, but they don't understand. Callista is a really nice girl with a decent, normal family. Our friends in Medanos are normal, status quo types—nice house, a couple of kids, a couple of cars. We're not identical, by any means, but basically we're all the same type—people with jobs, people who went to college, people who go to church. *Normal* people.

That's not us anymore. How would it look if Callista got back together with me? Wrong. Unless she *likes* answering questions about the guy with the drag queen dad, I think I'll do her a favor and stay away from her.

She'll understand it's a favor, eventually.

I walk fast, stretching my legs and shaking all the thoughts from my brain with my pace. After a series of long hills, the trail stops at the edge of the road. I cross to the parking lot and read a small sign announcing that this is Buchannan Valley College's East Lot.

The library is just a few buildings away. I push through the doors to find things busy and noisy. Groups of students sit at tables, working on projects, and every seat in the computer station is busy. I've spent hours in the library at school and at Medanos Junior College, scanning journals and magazines, formulating defensive arguments for all kinds of cases. It feels a little strange to be in a college library with no purpose and no deadline, but I find a couch in the periodicals section and dig in. It's a perfect distraction.

At first I just stick to what's around me—a random journal from a nearby shelf, the sports section in the local paper, the *New York Times*. Then I head for the computers and research "boarding schools"—and give that up when I realize how expensive most of them are. Mom and Dad will *never* agree to me leaving home for that much money.

When a group moves into the periodicals area, I snag a few pieces of recycled scratch paper and a golf pencil from a computer kiosk and settle into a study carrel in the silent basement stacks to write a letter. After the words *Dear Callista*, I cross out sentences and whole paragraphs as I attempt to explain about Dad, about the way things have been. It comes out sounding like a policy debate defense, full of evidence and argument and nothing I really feel.

I wad it up and sit staring for a while, feeling tired.

You can't force people to react like you want them to. You can't create a way to think about things that don't even cross most people's minds. No matter what I try to say to Callista to make it better, the obvious truth remains: Dad is coming home, and eventually, Callista will find out about him. And freak.

But what's the worst thing that could happen?

One of Mr. Lester's little tricks in forensics for breaking through our panic about having to speak in public was to have us freewrite for two minutes on the worst things that could happen to us during our event. Afterward, we divided our lists into two categories—legitimate worries and stage fright/paranoia. It turned out that, as a group, we were a lot more paranoid than we thought.

Okay, yeah, we could trip on the way to the platform, lose all of our evidence cards five minutes before an event, knock over the team's water pitcher, stutter, lose our voices—but chances are that even if one of those things happened, it wouldn't be that big of a deal. We all trained so hard for our events that most of us could rattle off our points blindfolded or if wakened from a sound sleep.

I remember laughing as Mr. Lester read our Worst lists out loud. Writing them really helped; none of the stuff I've dreaded has ever happened during an event.

Okay, so I never imagined Dad walking into the auditorium in drag. But none of the stuff on my *actual* list ever happened.

I turn over a fresh sheet of scratch paper.

What's the worst thing that could happen with Callista?

Slowly, the words come to me.

She could stop speaking to me.
She could out Dad to her friends.
She could decide to make us her missionary project and
   be scary-nice.
She could act like she doesn't notice and secretly talk
   trash about us.
She could . . .

It doesn't take long to run out of ideas. I cross out a few stupid ones as paranoid—really, Callista's not going to beat me up or get someone to run me down in their car. She can't *make* me feel any way, and she can't do anything I haven't already done to myself.

Didn't I already stop speaking to Callista—to protect myself from when she decided to stop speaking to me? Isn't Dad getting ready to out himself? All of my biggest worries have to do with embarrassment, humiliation, and fear—and just like during a forensics event, none of that is anything I can do anything about, except breathe and live through it.

Which completely sucks.

I draw a line under my list and write another one.

What's the worst thing that can happen in Medanos?

Immediately the list looks more realistic and less paranoid.

People could ask Pastor Max to make us leave church.
We might get kicked out of school.
Mom could lose catering jobs.
People could vandalize our house.
People could harass Dad.

People could hurt one of us.
People . . .

It would really hurt all of us to be asked to leave our church. It would be hard on Mom not to hang out with her Girls' Night Out women's group. I can't see Pastor Max deciding that we're a bad influence, but I know a few conservative families get wound up about things and like to control how everything looks at church. Dad coming down the center aisle in Mom's old linen suit would really freak them out—and me too.

Would Pastor Max ask us to leave? Would Dad even do that? If we get asked to leave a church, it's not like that changes God's mind about us. And we could always join another church.

I leave my first worry with a question mark next to it.

I cross out my second worry. Unless Ys and I do something to break school rules, we can't get kicked out of school because of Dad—unless the school wants to deal with Poppy and the American Civil Liberties Union. No one wants to deal with Poppy when he's in lawyer mode.

The third worry is realistic—people might decide against having Mom do their catering because of Dad. Mom's business could lose money, and she might have to work harder and lay off her staff.

This really scares me for a moment, before I realize something: Mom might also *gain* new clients because of Dad. It's a weird thought, but a good one. Maybe someone would feel safer with Mom because she's married to Dad.

The next three worries on the list are just too real. I hear in the news all the time about violence against gay and lesbian people. It gives me a stomachache to think that Dad is putting himself out there by being transgender. Someone could hurt him—or Mom—or Ys. It makes me sick with fear and anger.

I want to get online and find statistics for our state, for our city. Have there been any recent incidents? Do we live in a bad area for violence against gay and lesbian and transpeople? Should we move?

I stretch out my legs and prop my feet on the chair across from me, thinking hard. There has to be *something* we can do to protect ourselves. Does en|GNDR have resources for self-defense classes? I don't realize I'm drumming my fingers until I earn an annoyed look from the guy browsing the shelves next to me.

Shut it down, Justin.

I reach for my pencil again.

Fact: Random violence happens—no matter where you live.

Fact: Some racist could attack us for being African Americans. But no one has.

Fact: These last three questions probably fall at least a little under the category of "paranoid." Who are these "people"? Why do they suddenly know who we are and what we're doing?

Other than asking Dad to be careful and praying for him like always, there's nothing I can do about any of this. Just like every other day of my life, when I say goodbye to Dad when he flies down to supervise a building site, when Mom has a late job and I go to bed before she comes home—all I can do is make sure they know I love them, say my prayers, and let it go.

Stuff happens. None of us control anything.

"The library will be closing in ten minutes," a nasal voice interrupts, and I frown. Closing? What time is it? I have no idea how long I've been here, pulling one idea out of the air, rejecting it, pulling out another one. Standing, I pat my pockets for my phone to check the time and realize I don't even have my backpack. I shrug. I didn't know how long of a walk I was going to take, so everything is back at Dad's.

Folding my notes into a little square, I shove them into my back pocket, then visit the bathroom. It's good to move; I didn't realize I was sitting still for so long.

I splash water on my face in front of the mirror, feeling a little better. Even though I know I haven't solved anything—the Callista issue and all the other worries are still there—I don't feel so stressed. It probably won't last, but for the moment I feel okay.

It's like policy debate—most people hate it, because it takes tons of research, and there's a three-minute cross-examination session at the end of each speech. Policy is my favorite type of debate, though. I know how to dig in and find solid facts that make the argument for whatever plan I propose. It makes me feel better to nail things down with logic.

Stretching, I climb the stairs from the basement stacks and blink when I hit the main library floor. It's dark out, and the big clock behind the checkout desk says it's five till midnight.

How long have I been gone? I hurry toward the entrance, glancing around for a pay phone, but I don't see one. I pass a security guard in a plain blue uniform who gives me a brief nod.

"Got some good studying done?" he asks.

"No. I was thinking," I say, then realize how dumb that sounds.

"Thinking's good," the guard says mildly. "You need an escort to your vehicle?"

"No, thanks. I walked." I hurry past and push open the exit door.

Cars are streaming out of the lot. I head for the back lot, then change my mind; the lot is well lit, but the walking trails close at sunset, and I'd never find Dad's house that way. I'll have to figure out a long way around.

I sigh and shove my hands in my pockets, ignoring my growling stomach. Now that I think about it, I'm hungry. Did I even eat lunch?

Midnight. *Unbelievable.* Dad's going to be pissed.

I frown, picking up my pace. If I get home fast enough, maybe no one will notice I've been gone. Our curfew during a school break is midnight, anyway.

"Justinian Nicholas?"

I jump, turning to find the speaker. The same security guard is standing next to his open car door, engine idling. He raises his eyebrows. "Justinian Nicholas?" he repeats.

"It's Justin," I tell him.

"Thought so." The man nods. "You look a little young to be a freshman."

"I'm taking junior classes." I blurt the non sequitur. "Who are you?"

"You might want to call home. The police have been keeping an eye out for you."

"*What?!* Oh, crap." I pat my pockets and remember. "I don't have my phone."

The security guy just smiles and pulls out his radio. "This is

549 to base. Ronnie, you wanna call in to the PD that I've got their missing minor in front of the library here? Over."

The radio crackles, and a staticky voice says something garbled. The security guard nods. "Yep, safe and sound. We'll just wait for that black-and-white. Over."

That's it, I'm dead. I am *so* dead.

Happy Together

Ysabel

I'm relieved when Connor and Madison arrive. The stifling quiet isn't helping any of us, and with company, Mom has an excuse to dig into the back of Dad's pantry for a bag of flour and make sugar cookies.

Connor comes straight over and wraps me in a tight hug, his usual cheerful expression absent. "You okay?"

"I'm getting better," I say, manufacturing a smile.

"I'm sorry about Maddie, but she wouldn't let me take the car by myself," he says, giving her an irritated glance. "It was either both of us or no one."

"That's okay," I say, leading him into the living room. "Do you want something to drink? Mom made cookies."

Who knew that under pressure, the Nicholas family turns into a well-oiled hostessing machine? Dad brings out coffee and a pitcher of iced tea. Mom assembles a tray of cheese, crackers, and raw veg, while I transfer the warm cookies to a plate and slide the next batch into the oven. Dad makes small talk with Madison while Mom brings Connor iced tea. It feels strange to be smiling and passing around cookies when my stomach is twisting, and every time I go into the kitchen, I look at the microwave clock.

If Justin's not dead, I am going to kill him. It's been hours. *Hours.*

Then dread reverberates in me. He could be dead. What if he killed himself? What if he got hit by a car? What if—

I can't sit still. Even after everyone has something to drink and their snacks in front of them, I pace.

"Ysabel," my mother finally says, giving me a look. I perch on the arm of the love seat next to Connor and try to pretend that my nerves aren't twitching.

I can't stop watching Connor's Maddie. Her wavy blond hair is shot through with streaks of lighter blond and pulled back from her face with a satin band that matches her denim skirt and gray-blue eyes. When she smiles, I see where Connor gets his looks.

She reaches for a cookie and our eyes meet. My smile is embarrassed.

Madison's face is kind. "I've heard so much about you, it's nice to finally meet you, Ysabel."

"Thanks." I clear my throat. "I was just noticing how you and Connor look exactly alike." I wince, realize how bad that sounds. "I mean—"

"If you ever see a picture of me at his age, you probably won't be able to tell us apart," Madison says, and smiles at her son. "Connor's a much easier kid than I was at sixteen, though. I was always in trouble."

I smile nervously, and we lapse into an uneasy silence. I wonder if there's any polite way to ask Madison what she's heard about me.

"Bel, why don't you show Connor your torchwork?" Dad suggests suddenly. "You two shouldn't have to sit in here with us old folks. Go downstairs for a while."

"Good idea—take some cookies with you," Mom says, loading up a napkin.

Old folks? Yeah, I've heard this one before.

Connor takes the hint and silently follows me downstairs. He gives me a bewildered look as I grab the bathroom door in passing and close it loudly.

I wait for muffled voices upstairs, but there's nothing.

"What are you doing?" Connor finally asks.

I shake my head and continue down the hall into my room. "I thought they sent us down here because they wanted to talk. They're sitting up there not saying anything."

"Oh." Connor moves my bead catalog out of the way and sits on the bed. "You're as bad as Marco. He stands by his sister's door and listens when she's on the phone."

"Well, that's rude." I kick off my shoes and sit at the top of my bed, setting the cookies between us. "I only do it to my parents when there's something they're not telling me that I need to find out."

"That's what Marco says, too," Connor laughs.

I lean my head back against the wall and sigh. "I was

187

hoping they know something they wouldn't say in front of me, I guess."

Connor winces, his mouth pulling down. "I'm sorry about this, Ysabel. It feels like it's my fault."

"I don't see how it could be your fault. You didn't tell him to take off."

"I know, but—"

"Not your fault," I repeat, getting off the bed. "Here," I say, leaning over to pull out my box of beads. "This is what my Dad wanted me to show you."

"Those are—"

The doorbell interrupts.

I'm up and out of the room before he can finish.

"Justin, thank God!" I hear my mother's voice. "Where have you *been*? Do you know what you put your father through?"

"Don't be too hard on him," the policewoman is saying as my father grips her hand. "Losing track of time in a library is probably a sign of genius."

"No, it's not. Idiot," I mutter, leaning against the living room wall, light-headed and close to tears. *Thank you, God.*

Justin's eyes meet mine. "*Sorry,*" he mouths, giving me remorseful puppy eyes.

"Next time, son, take your phone," Dad interjects, relief in his voice.

"You didn't have to come," Justin says to my mother, who is glaring at him, her hands on her hips. "I'm so sorry, you guys. I was in the junior college library, and I must have zoned. I was just thinking, and I didn't realize how late it had gotten, and I forgot my phone—"

"You were 'thinking' and you 'forgot.'" My mother makes air

quotes. "When you figured that out, you should have found a pay phone, immediately. You know that, Justin."

"Uh, Connor and I are going to get out of the way now," Madison tells Dad, wading through the chaos to follow the officer out. "It was nice to meet you, Ysabel, Stacey. Justin, we'll see you next time."

"Connor! Man, I'm sorry," Justin says unhappily, looking around. "I didn't mean to worry everyone."

"We're good," Connor says, looking relieved to be edging away from Mom's tirade. He gives us both a wave. "Talk to you later."

"So, you just walk out of the house without saying where you're going?" Mom rails, undeterred. "Since when is that acceptable? Have you lost your mind?"

"Stacey," Dad begins, but he's fighting a smile. Mom's rants are kind of legendary. She rarely loses her temper, but when she does, it's hard for her to get it back.

"I just want to know—is this a onetime occurrence, or are we looking at getting one of those tags for you like vets put in puppies?"

"Mom!"

"Well, I just want to know," my mother says, throwing up her hands. "If you're going to be disappearing all the time, I want to be prepared. We'll get you a name tag. We'll assign someone to walk you home from school. Justinian Nicholas, if you ever scare me like this again, so help me, God—" Mom finally takes a big breath and just shakes her head.

Justin hesitates. "It . . . I just had to think," he says awkwardly. "I'm really sorry."

"Well, what—" Mom begins, but Dad slips his arm around her.

"It's late, Stace," he interrupts. "I'm sure Justin's hungry, and we'll have time to discuss this tomorrow, all right?"

"I'm starving," Justin admits.

"I need tea, then I'm going to bed," Mom says wearily. "It's been a long day."

"Mom, I'm—"

"Enough. Shush," Mom says, calm and reasonable again, leaning on Dad. "Bel, do you want a sandwich too?"

"We can manage," Dad says, turning her around. "Go on to bed, Stace."

"Ysabel, help me put away the food, would you?" Mom says, ignoring him.

I go help, wondering where Mom is going to sleep—or if it even matters.

Dad and Justin make tomato and cheese sandwiches I'm too tired to eat. Mom hunches over her tea, blinking slowly, while the rest of us pick over our meals in silence. All four of us are sitting in our regular places, just like we do at home. We might as well have never been apart.

"You can beat me up tomorrow." Justin's voice is muffled by his mouth guard.

"I still might beat you up tonight." I turn over and press my face against the cool side of my pillow. "Just because Dad made Mom put it off till we get to Hoenig's office doesn't mean I will."

"I can't believe Mom came up just for this. And Connor and his dad!"

"Justin, don't be dumb. You were gone something like eight hours."

"I know, but I didn't think—"

"*Ding! Ding! Ding!* Correct! Give the man a prize."

A deep sigh from the floor. "All right. I deserve that."

"You deserve worse, butthead." I flip over on my back. "You scared me."

"I know. I suck."

"Yes. Yes, you do."

"I'm sorry, Ysabel."

"Whatever."

"You know you love me."

"So? I'm still going to off you in your sleep."

"What*ever*. Good night."

"Night."

Dr. Hoenig grins. "Have the Nicholases had enough sleep and enough breakfast?"

I snort as we file into the therapist's office. "We're chronically sleep-deprived," I tell her. "There's also one more of us now."

"You must be Stacey," Dr. Hoenig says, beaming at Mom, who smiles back a little nervously. "It's nice to finally meet you in person," she adds. Justin and I exchange a look. Of course Mom has talked to Dr. Hoenig.

"So, you're still sleep-deprived, huh? Any other feelings this morning?" Dr. Hoenig asks, looking around the circle.

"Happiness," says Dad. He looks like a lazy lion, lounging on the couch and taking pride in his pride. "It's good to be together."

"Justin?" Dr. Hoenig asks.

"Uh, stupidity," Justin mumbles, and I snort.

"Stupid isn't a feeling; it's a state of being."

I twitch when Mom pinches me, but that doesn't stop my grin. Justin glares at me.

"*Ahem,*" Mom says, giving me a dire warning look. "I'm feeling hopeful."

"Hopeful?" Dr. Hoenig asks, sitting back. "Can you say more?"

Mom nods. "Today, things just feel—possible. It really is good to be with my family."

Actually, it's kind of weird to be with my family. We had breakfast this morning—on the run, practically, but together—and I realized just how tiny Dad's town house really is. Almost running into each other as we got ready, we barely made it out the door before Dad got agitated and started tapping his watch. With Justin and me racing to homeroom every morning, Mom doing catering mostly for lunches, dinners, and weekends, and Dad on the road so much, we rarely leave the house all together, unless we're going to church.

It's strange to feel that church feeling, here in Dr. Hoenig's office. I guess I'm beginning to equate the four of us being together to a religious experience.

That makes me snicker again. Inevitably, Dr. Hoenig focuses her red-framed gaze on me. "Sounds like you're feeling happy as well, Ysabel?"

I flick a glance around the room, taking in my mother's exasperated expression, Dad's faint smile, and Justin's annoyed eye roll. I shake my head, wondering at the laughter that bubbles up again.

"Happy," I say, considering the word. It carries no answers and no instruction manual, but it feels right.

Out of the Box

Justin

None of us feel like hiking today, which was what we were going to do at Jonas Wood. Instead, we talk Mom into staying another day, and just laze around the house.

Mom spends a long time Thursday afternoon on the phone, checking in with a client, making sure all the loose ends are tied up with a business lunch she's supposed to cater and generally checking in with the staff at Wild Thyme. When she's finished, there's a little lull in the action as Dad cleans the kitchen and Mom sits at the dining room table with Dad's laptop.

I don't actually mean to eavesdrop. Ysabel needs more darks

to throw in the wash, so Mom volunteers her jeans and a few of Dad's sweaters. On the way back downstairs, I pass my parents in the kitchen.

"You must never shop." Mom sounds reproachful. "I can't believe how empty your cabinets are. You're as bad as you were in college."

"Actually, I'm worse," Dad admits. "It's harder to eat my own cooking now."

"You have no onions," Mom exclaims. "How am I supposed to make anything?"

"Can't we just go out?"

"From the look of the takeout containers in your fridge, you *always* go out. Don't you cook anything yourself?"

Dad laughs. "Honestly, Stace? I try not to get home until I absolutely need to crash, and I don't even go into the kitchen until I make coffee the next morning. Most of the time, I get a sandwich at work."

"You're digging your grave with your teeth." My mother sounds irritated.

"So, will you stay here and cook for me?" Dad asks lightly.

"You're not taking this seriously, Chris," Mom complains. "There's not a vegetable in this house. You're going to kill yourself eating like this."

"Well, by all means, let me go get changed, and we'll find some vegetables."

I expect Mom to call downstairs for Ysabel and me, but she doesn't, so I go upstairs again. She's standing by the sliding glass door, looking out at the view of the oaks from the back of the town house.

I glance at Dad's closed bedroom and frown. "Mom?"

"Mm?" She sounds distracted.

"Have you ever seen Dad in Christine clothes?"

Mom turns, suddenly focused on me. "Mm-hmm."

"Oh." I stand next to her and squint out into the sunny afternoon.

An arm goes around my waist. "Have *you* seen Dad as Christine this week?"

"No. But he said he didn't want to do that this week."

She waits a moment. "Are you thinking about something specific in regard to Christine, or is this just general worrying?"

I shrug. "Nothing specific, just . . . do you ever think about what it's going to be like the first time we all see him? Or the first time Serena and Caleb see him at Wild Thyme, or the first time with people at church? Or . . . anybody? Do you know what you're going to do?"

I feel my mother's rib cage expand as she takes a deep breath. "No."

"No?"

"I have no idea what I'm going to do," Mom says. She smiles, a quick, amused grin. "Did you think I had everything planned out?"

"Well, no, but—yeah. I guess I thought since you were letting Dad come back, you had it all figured."

A little frown appears between Mom's eyes. "Justin, I'm not 'letting' your dad come back. I never wanted him to leave."

"Weren't you the reason he decided to stay here?" I look up.

Mom shakes her head. "His decision. Entirely."

"Well, that was—" I struggle to find a word.

"Painful? Typical?" Mom sighs. "He was trying to make it easier on us."

"But I'm not sure things can *be* easier."

"And that's why you're my smart son." Mom smiles. "Go get your sister. We're going out to lunch."

The Thai restaurant Dad takes us to is filled with bamboo plants, splashing fountains, fish tanks, and statues and shrines behind the counter. Horrible easy-listening plays in the background as the hostess, in a gold-embroidered outfit, takes us to a back room to remove our shoes. Awkwardly barefoot and a little cold, we follow her up a short flight of stairs into the carpeted loft, separated from the lower tables by an intricately carved wooden banister.

The hostess seats us at a table overlooked by a large golden Buddha. Dad sits first, easily dropping to the floor. The wooden coffee table where we'll eat is centered over a rectangular hole in the floor where our legs go. Dad scoots to the cushioned seat nearest the wall, leaving Mom the one closest to the aisle. She kneels on the floor to sit next to him, then laughs as she pitches forward trying to get her legs under the table.

We page through the menu, trying to figure out what's good. A man bustles up with a tray of glasses and a sweating pitcher of ice water, garnished with wedges of lime and a sprig of basil. Mom starts asking him questions, and I tune her out as the waiter pulls a pad from the waistband of his apron and answers her. He's scribbling and smiling, and then he reaches for my menu.

I hand it back.

"That's it?" Dad looks miffed. "I was still looking."

"Well, I went ahead and ordered a bunch of stuff for us to share," Mom says, looking guilty. "You'll find something you like."

I just shake my head. Mom ordering for everyone like this is usually the cause for a small family war, since her idea of fun is to order the weirdest foods on the menu she can find. She calls it "eating out of the box." Today, not even Ysabel comments. Instead, she and Mom sit and talk about the outfit the hostess is wearing and whether or not the lanterns on the wall are real brass or just aluminum. My father refuses to surrender his menu and keeps reading.

"Dad?" I ask.

"Hmm?" He looks up.

"So, when are you moving back home?"

My father sets down his menu. "Your mom and I have talked about that. Mom was looking at enlarging the closet and taking care of a few other things."

"Do you really have that many clothes?" Ysabel interrupts, abandoning her conversation with Mom.

"No, I don't have that many clothes," Dad says, looking slightly offended. "That's just one of the things we're doing to prepare. It's a lot of change to throw at everyone at once; we're just taking it slow."

"Well, I hope you're home before the Phoenix Festival," Ysabel says. "I'm thinking about showing some bigger pieces this year, and if Mom's got a weekend thing, I need a backup driver. Man, I can't wait till I get my license," Ysabel adds.

"We'll see how much driving school is this summer," Mom says. "I don't think my nerves can take anyone's driving but my own."

"Dad could teach us," I suggest. "You'll be home by summer, right?"

My father looks vague. "We'll see. Hey, here's our food."

The waiter sets a stack of plates and a rotating circular tray on the table. In the center are spinach leaves piled high and a bowl of sauce, surrounded by smaller bowls full of ingredients. "*Miang kum*," the waiter announces. Pointing, he identifies the diced contents of each of the small bowls around the spinach. "Chopped peanuts, palm sugar, fried tofu, dried shrimp, shallots, ginger, hot chilies, limes, and toasted coconut." He beams around the table and steps back. "Eat, enjoy."

There's a brief, expressive silence as all four of us stare at the mound of dark green spinach in front of us. Ysabel looks at me in disbelief, then both of us look at Mom, who bursts out laughing.

She stops quickly, her hand smothering the sound, but she's smiling as she watches us. "You should see your faces."

"This is going to be like the time you got us dim sum," Ysabel says plaintively. "Did you order anything we've had before?"

My mother gives her a exasperated look. "This is as easy to eat as a burrito, Ysabel. Just put a little of each filling on a spinach, add the sauce, and roll it up." Fumbling a bit, Mom makes a roll and hands it across the table to me. "Taste."

In the face of her forceful enthusiasm, I take a reluctant bite, wincing at the blend of sweet and sour spiciness exploding on my tongue. Ysabel picks up a spinach leaf and examines it closely, possibly for insect life.

"Try one. The only thing you don't want is the shrimp," Mom encourages her.

"That's not the only thing," my sister mutters.

Dad gives a pained smile and nibbles on a peanut. "Vegetables, huh?"

"Just try one." My mother hands another roll to Dad and looks across the table at me. "Isn't it good?"

We all make positive noises, and Mom turns to Dad, who shrugs. "It's great. You got some pad thai, though, right?"

My mother puts her head in her hands and groans.

* * *

After our dessert of mango and coconut sticky rice, Mom decides to take a walk to the Asian market at the end of the block and asks Dad to pick her up from there. Ysabel follows. I stand in front of the restaurant and wait for my father to pay for our food.

Dad is sucking on a mint from the bowl of candies at the cash register. He hands a candy to me, and I concentrate on unwrapping the brightly colored plastic, deliberately looking away from my father's face.

"So, do you not want to move back in with us?"

Dad hesitates mid-step. "What?"

I shrug uncomfortably. "Just wondering. Every time I mention it, you kind of dodge the question."

"I'm dreading being home alone Saturday night," Dad says, his brown eyes serious. "I don't know how I'll fill my time without you guys."

"Then why don't you come back with us?" I ask him. "Mom said she didn't even ask you to leave."

Dad looks away, his shoulders stiff. "She should have. Your mother is a saint."

I don't know what to say to that, so I don't say anything.

Eventually, my father exhales, a long, shuddering sigh. "You know how you keep your running shoes in the box they came in?"

I give Dad a look. "Yeah? What about it?"

"You want to keep them nice, right? You want to keep them pristine, so when it rains, you run on the paved track in the gardens at Heather Farm, right?"

"Um, Dad—"

"That's how I feel about my family," Dad says, his voice crowded with emotion. "None of this was ever supposed to touch you. You were just—"

199

"Supposed to stay clean in our box?" I ask, bewildered. "Dad, I don't see what that has to do with you moving back home."

Dad shakes his head, his face tense. "I can't do it yet, Justin. I miss all of you every day, but I can't change the way things are overnight. Do you understand?"

I open my mouth, but I don't know what to say. "I don't think any of us can change the way things are," I say finally.

"I know, Buddy," Dad says, looking away. "I know that better than anything."

Confused, I get in the car. Dad drives down to pick up Mom and Ysabel, and when we get home, he hands Mom the keys to the house.

"I'll be back," he says shortly. "I'm going for a walk."

"Do you have your phone? Make sure you don't get lost," Ysabel calls jokingly, but Dad just waves without turning back and disappears onto the walking trail.

"What's the matter with him?" Ysabel asks, but I'm still not sure. I do know that we need to keep talking in order to find out.

Mom settles onto the couch with the newspaper. I sit at the dining room table and wait for my dad.

At five, Dad calls and says he'll be late and not to wait for him.

At nine, Mom stands up and hands me the television remote. "It's all yours," she announces, and heads for Dad's room. "I'm going to bed."

Sometime after eleven, my fingers twitch as I feel the remote removed from my hand. By the time I open my heavy eyes, it's full dark, and a soft fleece blanket has been pulled over me.

I sit up. "Dad?" But I'm alone in the dark.

Happy Endings

Ysabel

It occurs to me that I might actually miss Dr. Hoenig, in the way that you miss a little splinter you had in your hand once you've dug it out. Dr. Hoenig is definitely like a little splinter. She didn't actually hurt that much, but just the annoyance of seeing her every day makes me glad that today is the last time.

Dr. Hoenig has out her lined yellow legal pad, and she's wrapping up her thoughts, talking about what we've said in the past and where we are now. We're just moments away from getting the heck out of here and heading to the beach.

Last night, Bethany phoned and invited us. She and her

dad organized our friends from the TransParent group, and we're having a going-away cookout. We'll build a bonfire and watch the sun go down on the Pacific. I'm all for big fires and sunsets, and I admit I want to see Connor when he's focused on me and not freaking about Justin.

I'm just hoping Dr. Hoenig lets us out of here sometime before I turn twenty-one.

"Dr. Hoenig, I'd like to ask a question," Justin blurts, and I make a pained little noise. *This* is why I try my hardest not to be in any of the same classes as my brother. His "one last question" is just the kind of thing he'd do during the last five minutes of the last class on the last day of school.

Dr. Hoenig smiles as I slide down the couch with a silent moan. "Sure, Justin. Shoot."

Justin glances at me. "We've told you what we wanted to get out of this week and what we got out of it. Would you tell us what *you* wanted us to get out of this week?"

The therapist looks surprised. "I'm not sure I understand the question."

I do. "He wants to know the point of talking to you."

"Ysabel," Mom says, frowning.

"I don't mean to be disrespectful," Justin interrupts. "I just know there was an objective to all of this, right? A goal. Did we make the goal, or what?"

I roll my eyes. Only Justin would check to see if we got the best grade in *therapy*.

Dr. Hoenig looks thoughtful for a moment. "As a therapist who specializes in transgender family therapy, I want my clients to be able to communicate about their needs, and my job, as I see it, is to help them bridge who they are individually and who they are as a family." Dr. Hoenig opens her mouth to continue, then stops. "Is that answering your question, Justin?"

"I guess," Justin says, then sighs. "No. Not like I wanted you to."

"What did you want me to say?"

"I thought you'd say that you were a therapist who helps families get back together."

Dr. Hoenig nods slowly. "That's a part of what I do, if the families are willing."

"Right." Justin's face is expressionless.

"So, what, you think we didn't meet our goal? Dad's willing to be back together with us, right?" I straighten, looking anxiously at my father.

"Right," Dad says, nodding. "Absolutely."

Mom, who's been very quiet, suddenly speaks. "The thing you have to remember, Justin, is that everyone has to find their own way back home, in their own time. Willingness is just the first step."

So, Dad is only willing? And "willing" isn't enough? Uneasy, I study my father, who is staring at the carpet pattern.

There's a silence—uncomfortable, since Dr. Hoenig is scribbling a little on the notepad she always carries, which means that there will be more over-observant questions next time. For a moment I'm apprehensive, and then I remember: this is my last session.

Which means her questions will all be for Dad. Good. For him, I have questions of my own.

"Well, we've made a lot of progress this week," Dr. Hoenig announces, closing her pad. She pushes to her feet and holds out her hand. "It was so nice to meet all of you."

Yes!

After the fastest goodbye I can manage politely, I practically gallop down the stairs to get away from Dr. Hoenig's office. I wait impatiently at the car for my parents to catch up, feeling a strange urge to move away from her office as fast as I can, to avoid finding out more things I'm not sure I want to know.

Justin reaches the car just ahead of Dad. "Are we leaving right now?"

"The beach at Goat Rock a two-hour drive," Dad says, pressing the lock remote. "We're going to take off at four, so we've got time to do some grocery shopping and run a few errands beforehand."

"Ooh, let's make hobo dinners tonight," Mom says. "I haven't done those in years."

Justin makes a face. "I'm sure there's a really good reason for that."

"Ha ha," Mom says dryly, and puts on her seat belt. "Hobo dinners are what we had in Girl Scouts. You take veggies, potatoes, and sausages, add some butter or mayo, salt, and pepper, wrap them in foil, and then bury it in the coals of the campfire. In about an hour it's done."

"Sounds good." Dad glances at me in the rearview mirror. "Belly, you need anything special for your dinner?"

"Just something with chocolate," I say, and lean back with a yawn.

"Oh, that's the basis of a vegetarian diet, all right." Mom shakes her head. "We might as well get the shopping out of the way right now."

After a quick grocery run we return to Dad's and unload. Mom gets me started measuring off squares of foil and scrubbing potatoes while she dices onions and carrots. Justin reluctantly cores apples with a newly purchased apple corer—Dad's kitchen seems to be lacking in all the little gadgets Mom likes—and packs them full of cinnamon sugar and butter to be wrapped and roasted.

"Real hobos would do this on the road," Justin points out.

"You're more than welcome, if you want sand in your teeth," I tell him.

Dad runs back to the store to buy a bundle of firewood, charcoal for the grill, and ice for the cooler. He's already packed up the sodas and his little grill by the time we're finished with the bulk of the dinner packs. Mom makes a plate of sandwiches, and we stop and eat a quick lunch.

"Don't forget to wear something warm," Dad advises as we grab blankets and tarps to protect us from the sand. "The fog is tricky this time of year: you never know how cold it's going to be."

"I'll get my sweatshirt," I say, and head for the stairs.

"Justin, you can borrow my old running shoes again," Dad begins.

"No, thanks," Justin says, crumpling his napkin. "I'll just wear mine."

Dad blinks. I burst out laughing. "Oh, *right*, Justin. You suddenly don't care if your shoes get dirty?"

Justin tosses his napkin into the trash. "As long as I can run in them, it doesn't matter either way."

"Well, they'll last longer if you keep them out of the sand and the wet," Dad says, still dangling the shoes. "May as well avoid replacing them as long as you can."

"They're just shoes," Justin says, looking away. "It's no big deal to wipe them off after I wear them."

"Okay, who are you, and what have you done with my brother?" I joke.

"There is no need to ruin your shoes just to make a point," Dad says roughly. "Just take the shoes, Justin, and let's load up the car."

"Dad, I don't *want* them." Justin's voice is low.

"Suit yourself," Dad says tersely. He disappears into his bedroom.

Eyes wide, I turn to Justin. "What was that? What point is Dad talking about?"

Justin scowls. "Nothing. I'm not trying to make a point. I'm just not going to be weird about my shoes anymore, that's all. It's not that big a deal."

"Well, how do shoes—" I begin, but Mom pushes a box of foil-wrapped corncobs into Justin's arms and shoos me downstairs.

"Ysabel. Sweatshirt," she reminds me.

"I'm going, I'm going. Hey, Dad?"

"Yep." My father reappears with an armload of sweatshirts and the hat Justin wore on the raft trip, looking grim.

"Do you have a little shovel or something if we want to make sand castles?"

"Think so," Dad says, brightening a little. He drops the clothes on the couch and heads for the garage.

Downstairs, I dig into the box of spiral flower beads I made. I didn't think to bring any ribbon with me, but a thin leather cord makes a decent hanger. I don't have wrapping paper, either, but I fold an origami envelope out of a piece of printer paper upstairs. I stick the package in the pocket of my sweatshirt and head for the car.

We're about to drive past the store when Mom starts her usual worrying. "Did you pack the salt?" she asks my father anxiously. "The pepper? Did you get the bottle of hot sauce off of the counter?"

"We've got everything but the fridge, Stacey," Dad says soothingly. "We don't have to feed the whole beach, and it's a potluck—other people are bringing things."

"I know." Mom leans her head against the seat. "It's just that when everyone knows you're a caterer, you want to make a good impression."

"Mom, nobody will care," I assure her. "It's a beach party."

"Remember the time Mom made that banana dish at the park?" Justin asks suddenly.

Dad chuckles, and Mom groans. "You guys aren't ever going to let me forget that bananas Foster!" she exclaims. "It's not fair to keep bringing it up!"

"But it was so cool," I protest. "You were the only mom at the eighth-grade graduation picnic who brought a dessert you could set on fire."

"Just because it was a picnic didn't mean it wasn't a special meal," Mom says a little defensively. "I just thought it should have a special dessert."

"It was special," Dad says. "It's not your fault the fire marshall had a niece in the graduating class."

"Nothing like a foot-high fireball over the rest of the food," Justin snickers.

"I still don't believe you need a permit to flambé food outdoors," Mom mutters.

Two years ago, summer, was when my biggest irritation was Grandmama saying my bathing suit was ratty and tight. I wanted to dye a blue streak in my hair once, but Mom wouldn't let me bleach it, and without the bleach, the color barely showed up. I had no idea about transpeople or gender identity, or Dad.

"That was a long time ago," Dad says a little sadly, putting my thoughts into words.

"Yes," Mom says dryly, "but not long enough."

"Fortunately, we have the rest of our lives to watch you make new and embarrassing memories we'll never let you live down." I yawn, leaning my head against the window.

Mom snorts. "Thank you, Ysabel. I am deeply reassured."

"That's what I'm here for."

A Trail of Bread Crumbs

Justin

"Hike!" Ysabel shouts. She throws the ball and Beth, in her trademark floppy hat, catches it and runs toward the water. A wave comes in and she shrieks, zigzagging away from the foam and back onto the packed sand.

"Tag!" shouts a woman with short, reddish hair, and smacks Beth's arm. "First down!"

Beth plants the ball, and the rest of the kids charge along the beach. I recognize Marco's little brother, who trips and knocks over another kid. The two of them roll around and get sandy, and for a few minutes, it turns into a free-for-all, with screeches and laughter.

I glance up the beach, watching Mom tend the fire. Between the driftwood, our store-bought kindling, and Mr. Han's big oak logs, we put together a pretty nice bonfire. There will certainly be enough food; even Dad was impressed by the number of boxes and bowls.

At the thought of my father, I look around until I locate him, in baseball cap and sunglasses, the legs of his jeans rolled. He's dragging Mom away from her fireside kitchen toward the surf. She seems to be arguing with him about this, and pretty soon, she's digging in her heels—for all the good it does her. Dad laughs as she breaks away from him and runs back to the fire. Score one for Mom.

Dad catches my eye and gives a brief smile before glancing down at my running shoes. I look down at my shoes myself, trying to picture Christine as someone who would drag Mom into the ocean, but I remind myself that Christine is Dad. There are parts of him that we will never lose.

"Viking!" The dark-haired woman scans the beach, shading her eyes. "Come play!"

"Be right there," Connor yells from behind me. I turn as he slogs through the sand in my direction. His legs and the bottom of his shorts are wet. "So, you don't do football," he says, and dusts the sand off his arms.

"I play. Just not in the mood." I shrug, looking out over the sparkling waves.

"Huh." Connor stands next to me, shoving his hands in his pockets. "You okay?"

"Yeah." I give him the lie, because there's nothing else to give him.

Connor turns to say something, then waves as the woman calls for him again.

"Viking! Come on!"

"Viking?" Ysabel emerges from the knot of little boys in the sand, balancing on one foot to try and dump the sand from her shoe. "As in, your other car is a longboat?"

"Ha ha. I picked up that nickname in Little League," Connor says, and gently kicks a hill of sand over Ysabel's other foot. He changes the subject. "When did you guys get here?"

"We've been here about a half hour or so." I glance back up the beach toward where my father is now turning food on the grill. "I had to dig Mom a fire pit."

"Your family are the most organized cookout people I've ever met," Connor says, grinning. "You actually brought a shovel? To the beach?"

"It's for a sand castle," Ysabel explains, sitting flat and dusting the sand from her bare foot. She looks up as the ball flies past, then surges to her feet. "Hey, I'm still playing!"

In the area of churned-up beach, the dark-haired woman steals the ball from Ruben and passes it to a little girl, who runs in the other direction with it. Pursued, the girl throws the ball back to the woman, who turns and wedges it between her knees and holds out her arms.

"Red light!" she shouts, and all the little kids stop running. Ysabel, in the act of freezing, falls over laughing.

I turn to Connor. "Okay, what was that?"

"Mom plays football by her own rules." Connor grins. "Come play."

"How am I supposed to play when I can't figure out the game?"

"It'll come to you," Connor says, smacking me on the shoulder.

We play a strange version of Keep-Away and Red Light/ Green Light, with the occasional down, pass, and wobbly punt involved. Ysabel enjoys the game until she drops something out of her pocket and screams for everyone to stop. There's a moment of ceremony as Ysabel retrieves a piece of jewelry and presents it to Bethany, who shows off the glass flower pendant and ties it around her neck. And then Mr. Han yells that it's time to eat.

There are a few last introductions as the people wipe off sandy hands and grab plates. Marco's mother, Mrs. Andrade, and his older sister, Sofia, are the makers of a pile of golden-brown empanadas, which Ruben and Marco's youngest sister, Lucia, claims she helped make. Connor's mom, who asked us to call her Laura, dishes out a chicken salad with grapes, almonds, and apples in it, which is surprisingly good. The Hans have brought deviled eggs, chili, and a massive fruit salad. Madison turns hamburgers, turkey dogs, and spicy hot wings on Dad's little hibachi grill, her long silver tongs moving quickly as she serves.

Ysabel follows Bethany to the edge of tarp furthest from the fire and pulls open her hobo dinner, fanning the steam away from her face. Connor and Marco follow. Sofia joins us for a moment but then has to drag a pouting Lucia back to sit with the smaller kids.

"How much older than you is Sofia?" I ask Marco.

"Three years. She's already a freshman at Stowe," Marco says through a mouthful of food. "Statistics major."

"Statistics." Ysabel winces.

"Exactly," Marco agrees.

Beth laughs. "You guys are such wimps."

"Just because you're a numbers person doesn't mean we have to be," Marco objects.

"I wonder if you can inherit that," Ysabel says. "Is your mom good at math, Marco?"

"Madison's a history professor," Beth says. "Connor aces history. Obviously inherited."

"That's bogus, Ys. Mom's a caterer, and you don't cook. Connor's probably only good at history because Madison would freak if he wasn't."

"Oh, trust me," Connor agrees. "She acts like it's the end of the world if I get a B."

"Mama's a nurse," Marco says gloomily. "If I was going to inherit anything, I wouldn't want the ability to stick needles in people and clean up—"

"Dude! Eating here," Connor warns him.

Marco says something rude in Spanish, and Connor answers. Bethany puts her hands over her ears and sings loudly. "I can't *heeeear yoooou*."

Ysabel chuckles. "You guys are so weird. I wish we had more time to hang out."

"I know." Bethany puts her hands down and pushes out her bottom lip. "I can't wait till your art show. Mom said we'll be there."

"Are we invited, too?" Connor asks.

"Um, anybody can come," Ysabel says, and looks pleased. "We have lots of room."

Sofia returns with a plate of empanadas, which Marco

steals. Ysabel interrupts their fight, asking, "So, Marco, your dad couldn't come today?"

Marco returns the empanadas and shakes his head. "Nope. He's somewhere in Argentina at the moment."

"Ooh, Argentina's on my bucket list," Ysabel says. "I'd love to go."

"I'm the only one of us that's ever been," Sofia says, snagging an empanada back from her brother's pile. "Our parents grew up there."

"Sweet," I say. "You at least always have a place to go on vacation."

Sofia snorts. "I wish. I can't afford airfare when I'm buying textbooks. Going home on the weekend is as much a vacation as I get."

Marco interrupts. "You could afford it if you asked Dad for the money."

Sofia's face tightens. "Which I won't. So, we're back at 'I can't afford it.'"

"Whoa. Sorry," I say, realizing I've stumbled into an old sibling argument.

Marco shrugs. "It's nothing. My father . . . can't deal with things right now. So, he's working for an import company in Argentina instead of living here. He sends money—"

"He just won't send himself," Sofia says, wiping her fingers on the napkin. She smiles a little. "I don't want anything from him but that."

"That sucks," Bethany says, grimacing. "It would be rough if my mom just . . . left, and stayed away. I'm sorry."

In the little silence that follows, I realize that Ysabel is looking at me, her expression troubled. I meet her eyes and give her a *What?* look, but she shakes her head slightly and looks away.

Sofia says, "For some people, it's impossible to live with being transsexual, I guess." She flicks a glance at her mother on the other side of the fire, talking animatedly to Mr. Han. "I'm taking a Gender and Culture Studies course at school, and our professor talked about how shame forces people into certain behaviors in this culture."

Connor makes a disgusted noise. "Shame sucks. If you couldn't talk to your wife, or your priest—I guess going away would make sense."

"He's just embarrassed," Marco mutters, and shrugs.

"He should be embarrassed," Sofia says, her voice sharp. "He's been gone so long Lucia barely remembers him. Who cares if he's not like every other dad in our society? He should come home."

Abruptly, Ysabel stands and heads up the beach at a fast walk.

I'm on my feet a moment later, jogging a few feet to fall into step with my sister. I keep my mouth shut, letting the boom and the hiss of the waves crawling up the sand fill the space between us.

Ysabel walks until the others are a ways off before she veers toward the waterline to pick up a half-submerged shell. She flings it sideways into the surf and stares after it. "Dad's doing what Marco's dad did."

I consider pretending I don't know what she's talking about, then breathe out a huge sigh. "Pretty much, yeah. Mom says it was all his decision to leave."

Ysabel picks up a rock, then throws it down viciously. "So stupid."

"Well." I hesitate. "We were pretty twisted for a while. I think we needed the space. Dad never meant for us to find out, Ys."

Ysabel shakes her head, still staring into the waves. "I don't mean *Dad's* stupid. I mean, I feel stupid. All this time, I kept worrying about him coming home and freaking out our friends. I kept feeling like we'd lost our father."

My stomach gives a guilty twist. "I know."

"I kept thinking, 'Man, what are people going to say about Mom? That she's a lesbian?' I couldn't stop thinking how people were going to look at me, you know? Then I got up here, and talked to him, and met Treva and Mr. Han and it didn't scare me so much anymore. *Dad* wasn't scary. He was just Dad. I thought, 'Okay. I can deal with this.' I figured I could work it out later if something else came up." Ysabel drags in a breath and shoves her hands in her pockets. "And all this time, he wasn't even planning on coming home."

"That's not true, Ys." I say the words as much to myself as to my sister. "He says he's coming home. Probably if we act like we expect him, he'll show up. We've just got to give him some time."

"How much time?" Ysabel asks, her voice rising. "I don't want to be like the Andrades, waiting for years." She looks at me, her eyes distressed. "I'm still not sure about Christine. I still worry about what people are going to say. But Dad staying away is wrong."

"Well, Mr. Lester says in order to defeat an opponent, you not only have to have a watertight argument, you have to deliver it in unexpected ways," I begin.

Ysabel interrupts furiously. "You want to have a debate? Now?"

I roll my eyes. "No. Mom says Dad needs to find his way home. We're going to figure out a way to leave him some clues. I don't know how yet either, but if we both think about it, we'll come up with something. I'm not willing to wait as long as Marco's family has."

Ysabel picks up another shell fragment and pitches it into the waves. "We miss him. I know he misses us. It doesn't seem like he'd need that many clues."

"Maybe he won't." I turn to see my parents walking up the beach toward us.

Happy Families

Ysabel

If this were a movie, my parents walking along the beach would be accompanied by some random piece of sentimental music, maybe with lots of violins. Dad grabbing Mom's hand would be Something Meaningful, and the angle of the sinking sun would make them blind to everyone but each other.

Unfortunately for all involved, this is not a movie. Dad walking toward me, all smiles and swinging Mom's hand, makes something inside of me twist.

How did things get so complicated? We all love my father—Mom does, even in ways I don't understand. Justin loves him, even though it freaks him out to think of Dad as a she. I love him, even though I admit I know it will be more than tough when I meet Christine. We all love Dad. Poppy and Grandmama love him. So why can't he just pack up his generic little condo and come back and live with us?

Why is he pretending he will?

"You guys done eating already?" Dad asks, pulling off his sunglasses to squint at us.

"What's going on?" My mother's observant eyes narrow. "Are you two fighting?"

"Why are we even here?" I blurt, which confuses both my parents.

"On Earth?" Dad laughs, but my expression shuts him down.

"You know what I mean. Why are you making jokes? I hate it when you make jokes," I say, frustrated. "I need you to be serious."

"Okay," Dad says, wiping the smile off his face with a wave of his hand. "I'm serious."

"You're not ever coming home, are you?"

Dad's brow furrows. "What?"

"I figured it out. You're going to just keep putting us off, and it'll be *years,* like Marco and Sofia's dad, and you'll just keep stringing us along, like that's okay, and it's not okay, Dad. I need to know, right now. Are you coming home? If you're not, just— don't pretend anymore, all right? Please."

My parents exchange looks, and Dad moves close to me. "Ysabel. I don't think you understand—"

"I'm not finished," I blurt, warding him off with a raised hand. I have to say this before I lose my nerve. "We didn't ask for this, Dad. Things were fine, and then we found out you were transgender, and we thought we would lose you, but then you were still Dad, and I thought that someday we were going to be okay. But it's not going to be okay, is it? Things are going to suck forever."

My mother sighs, and I'm grateful she doesn't voice her usual objection to the word *suck*. She wraps her arm around my waist, silently supportive. My father looks conflicted, his expression moving from stunned to angry.

"It's not low blood sugar this time," I add, defensive even though no one is speaking. "I just hate that we're all pretending. If you're not coming home, Dad, just say so."

There's a pause. Dad glances at Justin, who's stepped back a little, his arms crossed. "Well, Justin, since you started this, do you have anything to add?"

"He didn't start this!" I exclaim.

Justin shrugs, but his body language is stiff. "Hey, don't blame me. It's not my fault if the shoes don't want to stay in the box."

My mother steps between us. "Time-out a second—just wait."

"But—"

"Ysabel."

Impatient, I look off toward the water, watching a flock of gulls bobbing on the surface. Next to me, Justin shifts, his hands going into his pockets. I turn back to see my father watching me.

"Okay." Apparently our Mom-mandated moment of silence is over. "Nothing is going to be solved by shouting or accusing each other," my mother says, and I barely resist rolling my eyes.

"Sorry." Even though I'm not.

"I don't apologize. I didn't start this," Justin repeats, stubborn.

"All right. I apologize, Justin. Blame is uncalled for," Dad says, then heaves a heavy sigh. "Ysabel, I am coming home. If

I could give you three a date, I would," he says, pulling off his baseball cap and rasping the palm of his hand over his close-cut hair. "I know that's not the answer you want, but right now it's what we've got to work with."

"So, that still means you're coming home . . . 'someday,'" I say, making air quotes. Mom squeezes my shoulder.

"I'm sorry I can't give you what you're after," my father says tiredly. He closes his eyes. The laugh lines around them look like scars. "Everybody fears change, Ysabel. *Everybody*. Even me. This isn't easy. I've kept a part of my life to myself for as long as we've been a family. It's going to take time to work through that."

"How are we supposed to get used to Christine and everything if you're up here? When is that even going to start?" *How am I supposed to get past this, and just get on with my life?*

Dad shakes his head. "Belly, I don't know. I can't give you a timeline. But we'll get there, eventually. It just takes time."

"Okay," I say, defeated. I don't understand, but I try to smile. "Whatever."

"Belly," Dad says, and pulls me to him. He touches his forehead to mine, and I feel Mom's hand on my back. "I will come home, soon. I promise you. I promise *me*."

I blink hard, then pull back from what threatens to be a group hug. "Yeah, okay." I duck away from my parents and pick up another piece of shell.

Dad takes a deep breath. "Justin?"

"I'm good," Justin says, hands still in his pockets. Dad watches him for a little while, and I wonder what he's thinking. My father wanders closer to the water and finds a shell, and instead of throwing it, he hands it to Justin, who examines it. The two of them stand side by side, looking out at the water.

I throw another shell with more force than necessary. My mother glances at me sideways. "Still mad, huh?"

"No." I hurl more fragments at the sea.

"The hardest thing I've had to learn from all of this is that love doesn't force. We can't force your father to do what we want."

"I know that." I pick up a rock this time.

"He's angry with himself. He's ashamed of who he is right now."

My throw goes wild and bounces on the sand. "I don't want to talk about it."

"You know the chapter in Corinthians about love—" Mom begins, and I turn on her, my jaw tight.

"I know. I *know*. Mom, I have it on a teddy bear. 'Love bears all things.' I *get* it."

"No, you don't," my mother says, and her very firm hand on my arm stops me from throwing. "See if you can *listen*, Ysabel Marie. It's not just that love *bears* all things. It believes, it hopes, and it endures. A million broken promises, and love is still there, Ysabel. Love. Does. Not. Give. Up."

I look at Mom, and she nods, the set of her chin determined. "This family will not be giving up on your father."

When she lets go of my arm, I halfheartedly fling my last shell. Together we watch as it spins across the water and rebounds, making three effortless little skips before disappearing into the waves.

The sun dips toward the horizon in a smear of coral and pink, and we move toward the bonfire, which burns down the last logs in a shower of sparks. Laura brings out s'mores ingredients, and Beth makes me special chocolate-covered graham crackers, marshmallow-free. Madison wishes aloud that *someone* had a guitar. Marco shyly produces one from the back of the Andrades' minivan and plays.

When the fog comes in, the cold reminds us of home and warm beds. Mr. Han commandeers the shovel and smothers the fire, turning the coals in the cold, damp sand. Shivering, we carry the rest of the tarps and blankets back to our cars, and start the round of hugs and promises to keep in touch.

"It was nice to meet you," Sofia says, giving me a quick hug. "I'm sorry if I said something wrong at dinner."

"It wasn't you," I say, giving a quick glance toward the car, where Dad is talking to Mr. Han. "I just realized some things, and needed time to think."

"If you want to talk or anything, Viking's got our number," Marco offers.

"Thank you," I say, surprised and grateful.

Dad starts the car, and I look at Justin, who is leaning on the trunk next to Connor. Both of them straighten reluctantly and shake hands.

"Well, this is it, I guess," I say.

"Do you know when you'll be back?" Connor asks.

I look at Justin, who shrugs. "Nobody's said anything to me."

"Well. Phoenix Festival. Three weeks. That's not bad." Connor gives me a tentative hug. "Maybe Madison will let me drive down."

I hug him back as Madison says from behind us, "I wouldn't count on it."

"Come on, guys," Dad says, opening the car door. Beth hurries over for one last hug, and then we're down the dark road, the headlights behind us receding into a blur.

I want to cry. I feel like another thread linking me to Dad is coming unraveled, and pretty soon, we'll be on opposite ends of the state, and there will be nothing left of him.

Two minutes later, I get my first text from Bethany and laugh.

We're behind u! Cant get rid of us that ez.

I'm glad.

My father parks the car and insists on carrying my pink art case. He comes with us all the way to the security gate to say goodbye. There are people rushing around us, but that doesn't stop Dad from standing with us in a circle. With our arms linked, we hold each other as Dad prays, as he always does no matter where we are, when we're going to be apart. Eyes closed, I concentrate on the sound of his words, straining to memorize the cadence of his voice, as Dad prays for our safety. My own prayer is much shorter and to the point. *Please help Dad come home. Please. Please.*

We stand on the freckled tile, hugging. Dad kisses us good-bye. "I'll be down next weekend, if I can," he says, giving us one last hug. "Phoenix Festival, if not."

Mom leans against Dad and waves us ahead of her. "I'll catch up," she says. It is so hard to let go.

We move through security and replace our shoes and lug our bags along a corridor bright with shops. Justin walks slowly. At first I think he is waiting for Mom, but then he points at a coffee stand ahead of us.

"Think they have stamps?" he asks.

"What for?" I follow him to a postcard display, surprised as he selects a cheesy card of a local landmark and asks the seller for a stamp.

"Who's this for?" I ask.

"Dad. Have you got a pen?" Justin holds out his hand.

I dig through the pockets of my backpack and watch as Justin scribbles a single sentence on the back of the card and signs it. He holds it out to me, and I laugh.

Dear Dad,
Do you know that we love you?
Justin

I scribble my signature. On the bottom I add,

Tell Dr. Hoenig hi.

The seller points us to a little mail slot, and Justin inserts the postcard, shifting his backpack. Together we walk down the concourse toward our gate, heading home.

Nothing is settled. Nothing is "fixed," or right. On Monday, our family will still be separated, and Dad will still be both himself and someone else, mixed up between Chris and Christine. We'll never be the same family we were, ever again.

But maybe that's not so bad.

TRANSGENDER-SPECIFIC TERMINOLOGY, from GLAAD (Gay and Lesbian Alliance Against Defamation) Media Reference Guide http://glaad.org/referenceguide

Transgender

An umbrella term for people whose gender identity and/or gender expression differs from the sex they were assigned at birth. The term may include but is not limited to transsexuals, cross-dressers, and other gender-variant people. Transgender people may identify as female-to-male (FTM) or male-to-female (MTF). Use the descriptive term (*transgender, transsexual, cross-dresser, FTM, or MTF*) preferred by the individual. Transgender people may or may not choose to alter their bodies hormonally and/or surgically.

Transsexual (also *transexual*)

An older term that originated in the medical and psychological communities. Many transgender people prefer the term *transgender* to *transsexual*. Some transsexual people still prefer to use the term to describe themselves. However, unlike *transgender, transsexual* is not an umbrella term, and many transgender people do not identify themselves as transsexual. It is best to ask which term an individual prefers.

Transvestite
Derogatory. See **cross-dressing**

Transition
Altering one's birth sex is not a one-step procedure; it is a complex process that occurs over a long period. Transition includes some or all of the following cultural, legal, and medical adjustments: telling one's family, friends, and/or coworkers; changing one's name and/or sex on legal documents; hormone therapy; and possibly (though not always) some form of surgical alteration.

Sex Reassignment Surgery (SRS)
Refers to surgical alteration and is only one part of transition (see *transition* above). Preferred term to *sex change operation*. Not all transgender people choose to or can afford to have SRS. Journalists should avoid overemphasizing the importance of SRS to the transition process.

Cross-Dressing
Occasionally wearing clothes traditionally associated with people of the other sex. Cross-dressers are usually comfortable with the sex they were assigned at birth and do not wish to change it. *Cross-dresser* should NOT be used to describe someone who has transitioned to live full-time as the other sex

or who intends to do so in the future. Cross-dressing is a form of gender expression and is not necessarily tied to erotic activity. Cross-dressing is not indicative of sexual orientation.

Gender Identity Disorder (GID)

A controversial DSM-IV diagnosis given to transgender and other gender-variant people. Because it labels people as "disordered," the diagnosis of gender identity disorder is often considered offensive. The diagnosis is frequently given to children who don't conform to expected gender norms in terms of dress, play, or behavior. Such children are often subjected to intense psychotherapy, behavior modification, and/or institutionalization. Replaces the outdated term *gender dysphoria*.

Intersex

Describes a person whose biological sex is ambiguous. There are many genetic, hormonal, and anatomical variations that make a person's sex ambiguous (such as Klinefelter syndrome and adrenal hyperplasia). Parents and medical professionals usually assign intersex infants a sex and perform surgical operations to conform the infant's body to that assignment. This practice has become increasingly controversial as intersex adults are speaking out against the practice, accusing doctors of genital mutilation.

Transgender Terminology to Avoid

PROBLEMATIC TERMINOLOGY
PROBLEMATIC: *transgenders, a transgender*
PREFERRED: *transgender people,*
                    a transgender person
Transgender should be used as an adjective, not as a noun. Do not say, "Tony is a transgender," or, "The parade included many transgenders." Instead say, "Tony is a transgender person," or, "The parade included many transgender people."

PROBLEMATIC: *transgendered*
PREFERRED: *transgender*
The word *transgender* never needs the extraneous *ed* at the end of the word. In fact, such a construction is grammatically

incorrect. Only verbs should be transformed into participles by adding *-ed* to the end of the word, and *transgender* is an adjective, not a verb.

PROBLEMATIC: *sex change, preoperative,*
postoperative
PREFERRED: *transition*
Referring to a sex change operation or using terms such as *pre-* or *postoperative* inaccurately suggests that one must have surgery to truly change one's sex.

PROBLEMATIC: *hermaphrodite*
PREFERRED: *intersex person*
The word *hermaphrodite* is an outdated, stigmatizing, and misleading word, usually used to sensationalize intersex people.

DEFAMATORY TERMINOLOGY
DEFAMATORY: *deceptive, fooling, pretending, posing, or*
masquerading
Gender identity is an integral part of a person's total identity. Please do not characterize transgender people as "deceptive," as "fooling" other people, or as "pretending" to be, "posing," or "masquerading" as a man or a woman. Such descriptions are extremely insulting.

DEFAMATORY: *she-male, he-she, it, trannie, tranny,*
gender bender
These words only serve to dehumanize transgender people and should not be used.

Names and Pronoun Usage

We encourage you to use a transgender person's chosen name. Often transgender people cannot afford a legal name change or are not yet old enough to change their name legally. They should be afforded the same respect for their chosen name as anyone else who lives by a name other than their birth name (such as celebrities).

We also encourage you to ask transgender people which pronoun they would like you to use. A person who identifies as a certain gender, whether or not that person has taken hormones or had surgery, should be referred to using the pronouns appropriate for that gender.

If it is not possible to ask the person which pronoun he or she prefers, use the pronoun that is consistent with the person's appearance and gender expression. For example, if the person wears a dress and uses the name Susan, feminine pronouns are appropriate.

It is never appropriate to put quotation marks around either the transgender person's chosen name or the pronoun that reflects their gender identity.